The Alarming Palsy of James Orr

Tom Lee

GRANTA

Granta Publications, 12 Addison Avenue, London, W11 4QR

First published in Great Britain by Granta Books, 2017

This paperback edition published by Granta Books, 2018

A CIP catalogue record for this book is available from the British Library.

9 8 7 6 5 4 3 2 1

ISBN 978 1 78378 394 6 (paperback)
ISBN 978 1 78378 395 3 (ebook)

Typeset in Galliard by Patty Rennie
Printed and bound by CPI Group (UK) Ltd Croydon, CR0 4YY

MIX
Paper from
responsible source
FSC
www.fsc.org   FSC® C02047

For E de Z

Part One

I

WHEN JAMES ORR WOKE UP, A LITTLE LATER THAN usual, he had the sense that there was something not quite right, some indefinable shift in the normal order of things, but it was not until he bumped into his wife on the landing – James had been sleeping in the spare room for several weeks – that he had a clue as to what it might be.

'Oh!' said Sarah Orr, and put her hand to her mouth in genuine alarm.

James continued to the bathroom and there, in the mirror, he saw the cause of her dismay – and such dismay did not seem unreasonable.

The left-hand side of James's face had collapsed, a balloon with the air gone out of it, a melted waxwork. The cheek was hollow and the skin hung in a bulge over the side of his jaw, a grotesque one-sided jowl. The side of his mouth had fallen, too, the pale line of his lips angling sharply downwards. Where the bottom of the eyelid had pulled down, the full white of the eye was exposed, as well as its veiny roots. The skin itself was different. Yellowed, bloodless, and a little shiny.

James tried to smile. Only the right-hand side responded. The right eye narrowed, the skin creased into folds, the corner of the mouth hoisted itself upward and pulled his lips back over his teeth. The left side remained slumped, unmoved. The effect, a forced and crooked grin, the teeth bared on one side, was appalling.

Sarah stood next to him, staring at his reflection in the mirror.

'My god, James, what is it? Have you had a stroke?' She laughed, nervously. 'I'm sorry – you just look so… awful.'

James turned on the tap, splashed his face with water and then looked again. He put his hand to his face and it was like touching someone else. He pushed the left side up so that it was level with the right but it was not convincing, and when he let go, it dropped slackly back down.

'It won't move,' said James. The words came out thickly, caught in his half-closed mouth. 'It's paralysed.'

And yet it was not simply this, the sight of the paralysed features themselves, that was so unsettling, it was the discord between right and left. If both sides hung like this, then perhaps, at least when his face was at rest, he would only resemble a much older man – himself thirty or forty years from now. As it was, it gave the impression of two different faces, two different people, welded savagely together.

'Don't come downstairs,' said Sarah. She had recovered herself. James recognised the tone – practical, coping, in charge – most often employed when there was some kind of drama involving the children, a sound that he usually found reassuring. 'I'm going to sort out the kids.'

'Okay,' murmured James, out of the side of his mouth.

He turned back to the mirror. The only thing on the left-hand side of his face that moved was his eye. But when he blinked, only the right eye closed. The left stared unrelentingly back at him. Its gaze seemed agitated, intense, almost accusatory, as if all the expressiveness of that immobilised side of his face was now concentrated there. From downstairs, he heard the everyday noises of his wife and children having breakfast, getting ready to go out, sounds that suddenly seemed full of pathos, or at least a kind of anticipated pathos. The eye had a yellow, filmy look to it, almost as if it were sheathed in something else. The edges of the cornea were reddening. It felt dry and was already a little sore.

2

THE PREVIOUS EVENING JAMES HAD BEEN TO A neighbour's house for a meeting of the New Glades Estate Residents' Committee, of which, for the last eight months, he had been the chair.

They had run rapidly through the agenda: the long-awaited resurfacing of the estate road, problems with fly-tippers, problems with the gardening contractors for the shared land, arrangements for the summer party. There was some discussion about a resident who was having work done and who had left an overflowing skip in the street for weeks without it being picked up. James agreed that he would have a discreet word. William, a pedantic retiree whose two pairs of glasses hung in tangles around his neck, and who acted as the committee's neighbourhood watch officer, reported that there had been two further incidents of 'The Anti-Social Behaviour'.

The Anti-Social Behaviour was a euphemism for the sporadic discovery of teenage couples, assumed to be from the sprawling local authority estate half a mile away, in cars parked up at the far dead end of the estate road, by the entrance to the woods. Discussion of the problem was a favourite of the committee – in need of a vicarious thrill, Sarah had suggested to James – and several of them were very worked up about it. James had never witnessed it himself, although he had seen the beer cans, cigarette butts and fast-food wrappers that were sometimes left behind. Even if all the reports were accurate, which he doubted, he did not see that a huge amount of harm was being done.

'I have fed back to the police,' said William, looking up from his notes and replacing one pair of glasses with another, 'and they have assured me they will increase the number of patrols in the area as a deterrent. If anyone has any other suggestions, please say so.'

'There is a real danger,' said Vanessa, committee treasurer, 'that the estate will get a reputation.' Her voice, pained, nasal and complaining, never failed to set James's teeth on edge. As usual she was wearing too much of the gaudy, vaguely hippyish jewellery that he had heard she made in a studio at her house. 'Then we will be overrun. It's probably too late already.'

James had not even wanted to be on the committee.

With work and the kids he had enough on his plate already, but under pressure from his next-door neighbour, the incumbent chair, and with a view of himself as a good neighbour and a good citizen, he had agreed, assuming – not totally inaccurately as it turned out – that it would be a dispiriting assembly of time-wasters, busybodies, curtain-twitchers and NIMBYs. After each of the monthly meetings, James made Sarah laugh with impersonations of the other committee members who, in a discussion on whether to install a bike rack at the entrance to the adjacent woods, insisted earnestly and at great length on 'maintaining the architectural integrity of the estate', and who called for 'heightened vigilance' following the sighting of an unidentified hooded man walking along the road after dark.

After only a few months, the next-door neighbour had moved away and there seemed to be a tacit assumption that James would take over as chair. As he told Sarah at the time, he should have seen it coming. Since then, however, he felt he had run a pretty tight ship. The first thing he did was to establish a written constitution that clarified the committee's role and responsibilities. From then on the meetings were short and efficient. He kept a lid on the other committee members' tendency to digress and also tried to act as a corrective to the general air of parochialism and paranoia. At times this meant being rather abrupt, and initially this seemed to shock a couple of them, used to a more indulgent regime, but James was not doing this for fun, and soon enough he felt that most, if not all, of them came to appreciate his style. He ran meetings every day at work – he was a project manager at a medium-sized consultancy firm in town – and he sensed some deference to this professional background, as well as to his relative youth and energy.

Already James felt he had earned some credit, and passed a little test in his own mind, when, over the summer, a group of Travellers had held a series of loud parties in the woods. In recent years this had become an annual event, viewed apocalyptically by many of the residents, and along with the noise, the battered cars parked everywhere and rubbish strewn all over the place, there had been bad feeling that had threatened to spill over into something worse. James had urged a light touch, and had spoken with the apparent leader of the group, a spectacularly tattooed and frankly terrifying-looking matriarch, and when they moved on after only a few days, the woods were spotless.

James turned to Vanessa.

'Well, we must to try to keep things…' he began, but he was interrupted.

'I could rig up a few explosive devices? Booby traps?'

This was Kit, a new resident. He had moved in just

before Christmas, a few doors down from the Orrs, and joined the committee soon afterwards. He was about James's age, lived alone, and was constantly at work renovating his house. Over the past few months, as James came and went from work, and even when it was very cold, he had watched Kit sand down and repaint the external woodwork, re-lay the steps up to the front door and dig out the garden. On the days when he was not outside, the sounds of hammering, sanding and drilling came from within the house. James wondered what Kit did which allowed him to rarely – if ever, as far as James could tell – go out to work, and yet afford the house and the expensive-looking Audi that was parked outside. He meant the explosives as a joke, no doubt, but perhaps he did know how to do something like that, James thought.

'I wouldn't mind,' said Vanessa, coyly, and the rest of the committee laughed. 'But I would settle for some CCTV cameras.'

'As I was about to say,' said James, before Vanessa could go any further, 'we have to keep things in perspective. For now, I suggest we continue to monitor the situation. If there's nothing else, then let's wrap this up.'

As usual, the meeting dissolved into general talk and drinks. James often stayed just for one, out of politeness to whoever had been hosting that evening, but on this occasion he was tired and decided to go straight home. Sarah was already in bed when he got in, presumably asleep, so he watched the news for a few minutes and then went up to the spare room.

3

'REMEMBER LISA'S HUSBAND?' SARAH WHISPERED. 'Lisa who I used to work with? He had something similar a couple of years ago. I forget what it was called. Something palsy...'

James and Sarah were sitting in the packed Monday morning waiting room at the doctor's surgery. Already Sarah had dropped the kids off at school and the nursery and had called James's work to say he wouldn't be in and then her own work – a small charity – to say she would be late, and she was now searching for clues to his condition on her phone. James was feeling acutely self-conscious. He wished he had brought a hat that might at least obscure the left side of his face. When he had stood up and tried to drink a cup of water from the cooler it had dribbled straight out of his mouth and soaked into his shirt. He did not remember Lisa's husband.

'Ah, here it is,' she said. 'Bell's palsy. A form of facial

paralysis caused by a dysfunction of the cranial nerve. It results in the inability to control facial muscles on the affected side. That's you, I think.'

When they were called in, the doctor confirmed Sarah's diagnosis. Asked to explain what had happened, James struggled to get his words out. Sarah laid a hand on his arm and he fell silent while she spoke for him.

'There is the possibility of Lyme disease,' said the doctor, addressing Sarah, 'but as James has not been to any known risk areas recently, and hasn't had a rash, that seems unlikely. With a stroke, one is usually able to wrinkle the forehead, even on the affected side, and he doesn't have any of the other symptoms. We'll send him for the relevant tests, of course, but it's classic Bell's. I'd pretty much stake my reputation on it, such as it is.' She smiled at Sarah and then held the smile as she turned to James. He had met the doctor a few times before – once when the surgery had written to him the previous year, soon after he turned forty, inviting him for a 'health MOT', and also on the occasions when he had taken the children in. Rebecca Moffat, her name was. She was young, extremely tall, bony and grey-faced, never less than cheerful.

'It's a very odd thing,' said Sarah. 'I was quite shocked.'

'Yes, the effect is rather extraordinary, isn't it? But I

see it surprisingly often – usually in men, as it happens. We don't know why, but there you have it. Given everything we have to contend with as women – I'm thinking about childbirth, among other things – it doesn't seem that unreasonable. In fact, I had a boyfriend once who...' She trailed off, preoccupied. 'Never mind. The point is, the pathology is still largely a mystery. It's one of those conditions we can't exactly diagnose, we can only say what it isn't. Have you been particularly stressed recently, James? Anything bothering you at all?'

James shook his head, tried to smile, but then thought better of it.

'Well, that's something.'

Dr Moffat went on, talking to Sarah again now. 'After a while, you'll probably stop noticing it. It's amazing what we can get used to.' She turned to her computer and began typing. 'I'll refer you to the hospital for those tests. Then it will probably be steroids to sort you out. Meanwhile, let's prescribe some drops to keep that eye nice and fresh. Take some time off work. Rest is important. I'll write you a note. Come back and see me if you have any concerns.'

'It will get better though?' asked James, with difficulty. He had not meant to sound so desperate, so pathetic. Sarah and Dr Moffat turned to him, a little startled, as if they had forgotten he was there.

'Oh, yes,' said Moffat, recovering her enthusiasm, 'almost definitely. The vast majority start to get better within a few weeks. In the long run, only a small percentage do not return to more or less normal.'

'More or less normal,' said Sarah, and then laughed, briefly. 'I'll take that.'

By the time they turned back into New Glades, James was feeling a little better. What had happened was not as bad as it looked, or as serious as he had feared. It was an inconvenience, a bizarre inconvenience, that was all. He could already see himself describing it to people at work, how he had woken up with the face of the elephant man, making a joke of it – a few weeks or even a month from now maybe, but still. And he was buoyed, as he almost always was, by the sight of where he lived.

The New Glades Estate was, James still thought, a pretty unique sort of place. He and Sarah had stumbled across it one day, entirely by accident. They had already been house-hunting for six months and had had two properties fall through at the last moment. That afternoon, an estate agent had stood them up for a viewing. Their daughter, Laura, who was four years old at the time, was having a rare tantrum and Sarah, pregnant with their son Sammy, felt sick every time she stood up. Exhausted and fractious, they had taken a wrong turn on the way home and arrived on the estate. They drove to the end of the road in order to turn around and there was the house, with an estate agent's board outside it. It was empty, so they went up the steps and looked through the windows. A flock of parakeets that had been roosting in the cherry tree in the front garden flew up in a riot of exotic greens and yellows, delighting Laura, and they knew immediately that this was the place. Even James, not given to such declarations, told friends it seemed like fate.

New Glades was a sixties' development, built on an area of ancient woodland owned by a monstrously wealthy private trust. The forty-eight identical houses were stacked in four terraces up the side of a hill. Each had its own small gardens, front and back, and the rest of the land was communal, sweeping lawns landscaped around many of the original giant spruce trees. On two sides and at the bottom of the hill were the woods that the estate itself had been carved from. From the front of the houses there were views over the woods, north towards the city skyline. It felt like a world away, but, as James often told people, fifteen minutes on the train and you were in the centre of town, a journey he made every day to work.

Whenever it came out that he lived on a private estate, James was always quick to add 'it's not as grand as it sounds'. It was true that the term 'private estate' didn't mean much: a small sign to that effect at the entrance, a monthly maintenance fee paid to the trust and various antiquated regulations about the colour of the front doors and the style of the window frames that the residents had long since stopped paying attention to. The houses themselves were not particularly large and certainly not ostentatious, just well designed and full of light. They had been built, in part, from the trees cleared from the site, and there was some element of copper in the roofs that had given them a sheen of verdigris over time, as if they were slowly reintegrating with the organic environment. The relative modesty of the houses was one of the things James liked best, the democratic and egalitarian spirit of neighbours all living in equivalent homes, as well as this apparent sympathy with the original landscape. They had featured in magazines when they were first built, an example of the utopian spirit of the era, and had sold at a premium. These days, as the estate agent told them, everyone wanted to live in a Victorian villa with period features, and the Orrs picked the house up – the previous owner had died and left it to his sister, who just wanted rid of it – for what was undoubtedly a bargain.

It was hard to believe, James and Sarah often remarked to each other, but they had been at New

Glades for nearly two years. The kids were growing up there, they could not foresee a time when they would want to move, and, in James's mind at least, the house had taken on the sanctified status of a family home. He tried not to be sentimental, but he knew that when he and Sarah looked back on their lives, this would be one of the most significant places. Sammy had, in fact, been born there, in their bedroom, when Sarah had gone into labour so rapidly in the evening that there was no time to get to the hospital. Early the next morning, after a long night helping the midwives with the birth, with his son upstairs for the very first time, asleep on his wife's chest, James had stepped outside the front door and seen the most glorious dawn breaking behind the trees, the world seemingly re-made, and had felt full of life's infinite possibility.

And now, driving back into the estate – or being driven, with Sarah more or less observing the ten-mile-an-hour speed limit – on a crisp, bright, pale blue March day, the dark green of the laurel hedges flecked with the lime-green leaves of new growth, it was hard not to recapture some of that feeling from the first day of his son's life and – this was a little embarrassing – feel himself spontaneously and irresistibly well up.

Once they got back through the door, Sarah gathered up her things for work.

'Enjoy your day off,' she said.

'It's not exactly a day off,' said James.

Sarah looked over at him from where she was standing by the door and he saw that he had not spoken clearly enough.

'It's not exactly a day off,' he repeated, more slowly.

'Well, okay,' she said. 'Anyway, I'll probably think of some things you can do. I'll be in touch.'

When she had gone, James sat back down on the sofa and turned on the television. He flicked through the channels and then turned it off. He opened the laptop and stared for several minutes at the screen. He considered running a bath. After a while he went to the kitchen and put some bread in the toaster. When it was done he stood by the back window looking out, chewing it gingerly in the right-hand side of his mouth.

4

JAMES FELL ASLEEP ON THE SOFA IN THE LIVING room. He had not intended to. He never slept during the day. Apart from anything else, he never had the opportunity. He had eaten the toast, sat down to think about what to do next, and that was it. When he woke up it was nearly one o'clock. He felt groggy, out of sorts. It was still hours before Sarah arrived back with the kids, so he decided to go for a walk to clear his head.

As soon as he had crossed the road and gone into the woods through the gate in the laurel hedge, he felt better. He turned right off the main path and began to follow the track that ran around the perimeter of the estate and then pressed on up the hill. The crispness of the morning had resolved into a beautiful, almost warm day. Even in the woods James could feel it, and the light fell in hazy stripes and pools through the canopy. He took off his jacket and tied it around his waist. Every few seconds, from different directions and very clear, there was the staccato drumming of woodpeckers, a sound that, to James, always seemed full of an extraordinary hopefulness.

He cut left down a bank, skidding a little in the winter mud that had not yet dried up. There he picked up the route of a disused railway line along an embankment marked on either side by a procession of huge, gnarled oaks. In places the twisted metal of the old tracks emerged from the ground, and here and there, in the shade of the oaks, were patches of crocuses. Half a mile further on the track disappeared into a boarded-up train tunnel now colonised by thousands of bats. Local myth had it that behind the boardings, deep inside the tunnel and the bowels of the hill, was a train, abandoned there when the line was decommissioned a hundred years before.

James took the steep path to the right of the tunnel, climbed up around it and then doubled back over the top. He was not far from the western edge of the woods, its highest point, and he could hear the cars on the busy road that formed its border on that side. Here, among pine and fir trees, there were traces of huge Victorian mansions built by wealthy families up on the hill to escape the city smog. After the First World War they had become too expensive to run and were knocked down, their foundations ultimately reclaimed by the wood. There were sections of crumbling, moss-covered wall, enormous severed ceramic pipes, flights and half-flights of stone steps and, in one place, an unnaturally flat rectangle of space that was said to have been a tennis court.

Laura loved it up there and James had often taken her and her friends to scramble and jump and climb around the site. James liked it too, this evidence of earlier eras and ways of life accruing like geological strata, like the ruined terraces of some Mayan or Aztec temple system. He thought, among the rubble and the undergrowth and the bent and buried metal, about the trains steaming through, about these grand houses and their inhabitants, perhaps in their tennis whites or drinking gin on their verandas overlooking the city, the temporary-ness of these civilizations. It gave you a perspective, something transcendent, like looking out over an ocean or up at the stars and feeling your own smallness. The parakeets that roosted in the Orrs' cherry tree were said to be the descendants of a pair that had escaped from the aviary of one of the big houses when it was abandoned.

Some distance beyond the last set of foundations, ten metres or so off the main path and largely hidden in the trees and undergrowth, James could see the old folly. This was a Victorian oddity, originally at the far end of one of the gardens, a kind of small stone fort built in Gothic style as a ruin, three half-fallen-down walls, a broken arch and no roof, presumably for the entertainment of the children of the house. Laura and her friends were intrigued by it too, but whenever they went up there James always steered them away because, for as long as they had been at New Glades, there had been a man living there.

He could see now the ragged blue tarpaulin that was strung between the trees around the folly to provide shelter from the rain. On previous walks, with Sarah and the children, he had also seen clothes hanging from the surrounding branches, but James had never seen the man himself. He had been mentioned at the residents' committee a number of times when James first joined. William, the neighbourhood watch officer, had been concerned. Different things were said, wildly different – that he was an asylum seeker, Afghan or Iraqi, or a city trader who had lost his job, his family and his house, or some disturbed person who had been dumped out of a psychiatric hospital. The authorities – the council and the trust – knew about him, apparently, but the camp had remained there all year, through the freezing winter, and the one before. It all seemed improbable to James – a kid's story, the man who lives in the woods, like the train in the boarded-up tunnel – but there were the clothes, and sometimes the tarpaulin seemed to have been re-hung at a different angle. There were no clothes visible today and no other signs of life, either, but James was not tempted to investigate. It gave him an eerie feeling, the possibility of another human presence nearby but concealed, a sense that even in this public place he was trespassing, and he walked on.

When James emerged from the woods twenty minutes later the sun was blinding and it brought him to a stop. It took several moments for his eyes to adjust, and when they did he spotted a figure up on the roof of one of the houses, straddling the ridge of it, hammering away at something. It was Kit. He wasn't wearing a shirt and this struck James as an affectation. It was still only March, after all. James was just about to go on up to his house, to take the few steps that would put him behind the cherry tree and out of view, when Kit looked up, saw him, and waved the hammer in the air.

'Hello James,' he called.

James hesitated. He could not fail to acknowledge him. It would appear to Kit that James had been standing watching him, though this was not the case at all. On the other hand, he did not wish to be drawn in.

'Hello,' James called out, but he had forgotten about his mouth and it came out as a kind of strangled cry. He raised his hand and waved it, though he was not exactly sure if this was an apology for the sound of his voice or an alternative greeting, and then ducked under the cover of the cherry tree. It was annoying, somehow, to have been seen hanging around the woods in the middle of the day, and then to have fluffed the encounter so completely. He climbed quickly up the steps and let himself into the house.

5

A FEW DAYS LATER, ON FRIDAY NIGHT, JAMES AND Sarah were due at their neighbours, the Fullers, for dinner, an arrangement that had been made the week before.

'It's fine if you don't want to go,' said Sarah. 'I've let them know the situation, as it were. We can cancel the sitter.'

'No, no,' James insisted, 'life must go on.'

There had been no change in his face. He had been to the hospital, where they had run various tests and excluded the possibility of anything more serious. He was given a prescription for steroids and shown some exercises that would help rebuild the nerve endings. The first night, when Sarah arrived home with the kids, they had sat Laura down to explain what had happened and to tell her not to be worried about it. She was not worried. She was briefly interested when James showed her some of the faces he could make but started to fidget when Sarah began to talk about paralysis, nerves and regeneration. 'I know, I know, Mum,' she said irritably, as she did about anything that bored her, and then wandered off. Sammy, eighteen months old now, gave no sign of noticing any change. James found all this reassuring.

On the second day, he had phoned his work to update them. Deborah, his manager, had told him to take as long as he needed. 'You're no good to us like that,' she had said, 'I can't have you frightening the clients.' She had laughed in a friendly way and he had laughed with her, or tried to.

James tried to remain upbeat but life was suddenly more complicated, and the little frustrations did get to him. Eating and drinking were slow, messy and undignified. The same applied to cleaning his teeth and shaving. He put the drops the doctor had given him in his left eye every few hours but it remained sore, a persistent, burning presence. At night he taped his eyelid down as the hospital had suggested but by morning the tape had always peeled off and the eye was raw again. On top of this, he felt unusually tired and flat, as if the animation that had gone out of his face had taken something less tangible with it as well, and he continued to take long naps in the middle of the day.

*

'Good grief, James,' said Connie Fuller when she opened her front door. 'I thought Sarah was exaggerating.'

James grinned, his best monster grin.

'Is it painful? It looks painful.'

James shook his head.

'Just the eye,' he said, his mouth contorted in a way that he had found allowed him to best get his words out. 'Can't feel anything else. That's the problem.'

'Ah, the afflicted!' Greg Fuller had appeared behind his wife. 'My cousin's husband had Bell's. Connie, you remember Jeff? They're divorced now, actually, though I don't think the two things are related.' He put his hand on James's shoulder and smiled at Sarah. 'Well, Jim, they say we all end up with the face we deserve.'

'Do they?' said James, but the Fullers had turned and gone back into the house.

They lived four doors away on the same terrace, the Orrs' first and best friends on the estate. On the day the Orrs moved in, the Fullers' enormous wolfhound, Sidney, had run through their open back door and upstairs, scaring the kids. 'Apologies,' said Greg, who had rushed after the dog and dragged him back downstairs, 'he's a friendly bastard really.' Greg and Connie had stayed for a cup of tea among the Orr's half-unpacked boxes. They had three children, the youngest two the same age as Laura and Sammy, and had moved to New Glades a year earlier for much the same reasons as the Orrs. 'I like them,' Sarah had said after the Fullers had gone, 'and they like us,' and James had felt grateful to them for confirming his positive intuition about their new home.

Since then, the Orrs and the Fullers had been in and out of each other's houses on an almost daily basis. The Fullers were easy to be with. The kids all got along and Greg and Connie were warm, generous and disarming. They liked to eat and drink and argue, mostly with each other. When Connie was drunk she liked to say how much she disliked New Glades. 'How did I get here?' she said. 'Pushing out children and getting fat. I blame my husband.'

Part of the pleasure in being with them, James knew, was that he had a crush on Connie. She was not getting fat, at least as far as James could tell. She was wiry and athletic, her large, expressive green eyes and freckled cheeks partially concealed behind thick black-rimmed glasses. Her red hair, cut into a short fringe high up on her forehead, was shot through with grey. She was very tactile, sat too close or touched James's arm or hand when she spoke or was being spoken to, her eye contact absolute, a quality of attention that seemed just part of her natural vitality and vividness, rather than cynical or teasing. The result, of course, was that James often thought about what it would be like to sleep with her. He did not think there was any need to feel bad about this. Connie probably provoked the same feelings in many men. On top of which, Greg flirted shamelessly with Sarah, and she with him. It seemed to James that they were at their best when they were with the Fullers, and though they had never discussed it in this way, he felt that Sarah would agree.

In the kitchen a large casserole dish was already sitting on the dining table.

'Shin of beef,' said Greg. 'Underrated and therefore very cheap. I've been slow cooking it since this morning. Ideally it needs twenty-four hours, but I'm not some kind of maniac.'

For his birthday, a few months before, Greg's colleagues had clubbed together to send him on a weekend butchery course. Afterwards, he had described the various techniques in great and gruesome detail. Knowing how it was killed and prepared and its different cuts, he had insisted to James more than once, was a form of respect for the animal.

'Forgive the meat bore,' said Connie. 'I've come to the conclusion that this is just part of some embarrassing masculine crisis Greg is having. At least he hasn't run off with a schoolgirl.'

'Or one of the neighbours,' said Greg, and slid his hand around Sarah's waist.

James and Sarah sat down at the table. Greg carried over the plates and began to serve up the meat. Connie poured wine and added a straw for James. 'I bought them especially,' she said, and winked at him.

At first James was a little elated to be out and among friends, the most normal thing he had done in a difficult week, but the eating and the talking were hard work and gradually he lapsed into silence as the conversation went on around him. Sarah, Connie and Greg were talking about a holiday the two families were planning to take together in the summer. Connie's parents owned a farmhouse in France and it would be the first time they had all been away together. James did not contribute. He had been looking forward to the trip, but at this moment the idea of being on holiday seemed remote and unreal. He could not imagine himself sitting by the pool drinking small beers, enjoying a long lunch in a restaurant or strolling around French markets.

He was making slow progress on the dinner. The meat was tender but he was still having trouble chewing it down and when the bits got stuck in his teeth he could not get them out again. He also felt annoyed – he knew unreasonably – that beyond the acknowledgement at the doorstep, and the provision of the straw, there had been no further discussion of his face or concern at how he was coping. He felt it might be a form of pity or condescension not to mention it, rather than simply tact. He knew, equally, that he would have been annoyed if too much had been made of it.

The others had finished and after a few minutes Greg asked if they should continue with the dessert. James waved them on. Greg had made ice cream and it would be considerably easier to eat than the beef, James thought moodily, but he did not want to admit defeat. Meanwhile, he realised that the straw had allowed him to suck up a deceptively large amount of the wine that Connie had been keeping topped up. He was quite drunk, but not particularly pleasantly – dazed, woozy, tired again.

Sidney had wandered in and Greg began to pick bits of meat out of the casserole dish and feed them to him. If James could fault the Fullers on one thing, it was Sidney. He had nothing against dogs in general, but Sidney – huge, slobbery and undisciplined – was a menace. There was something a little conceited in having an animal this big, so impractical and expensive to keep, getting in everyone's way, like having a flashy car. He regularly escaped from the house or leapt the garden fence, ran around terrorising the smaller children and left his giant craps all over the estate. It had even come up at the residents' meetings and James had been put in the annoying position of having to defend his friends and then, later, ask them to get the animal under control.

Greg was teasing Sidney with a piece of meat and the dog reared up, put his front paws on the table and snatched it from his hand.

'Do you fucking mind?' said James.

He had intended this as a joke, but when he looked around he saw that it had not been taken that way. Sarah, Greg and Connie were staring at him in surprise and, it seemed, in dismay. Perhaps it was the lack of control over his mouth, or the muffling effect of the meat still caught in there, that had made it come out more aggressively than he had meant it to. Or perhaps his facial expression, no longer a reliable guide to his feelings, had given a false impression of his intent. But it was also true that he did mind. He was still eating himself and to have the dog slavering away noisily next to him – well, it was too much.

'James!' said Sarah, after what seemed like a long and awkward silence.

'I was only—'

'James is right,' Connie said, cutting in. 'It's disgusting. The dog gets away with murder. Greg, you need to train your animal.'

'Now, Connie. If you remember, it was you that wanted…'

The Fullers began to bicker with each other. James saw that they were trying to offer a distraction from his outburst, to save him from embarrassment, and that he should be grateful for that – but, for some reason, he was not. It took him another fifteen minutes to finish his food and when he finally laid down his cutlery he was exhausted. He declined Greg's offer of ice cream. A few minutes later Sarah said she thought they should get back and, thanking the Fullers, they left.

At home, James left Sarah downstairs paying the babysitter and went straight up to the spare room. Despite his tiredness, it took him a long time to get to sleep.

6

WHEN HE WOKE UP THE FOLLOWING MORNING, James felt better. He rang the Fullers to apologise. Connie answered the phone. 'Don't worry about it,' she said, 'Greg was being a dick. I've already told him.' Then, in the afternoon, when Laura had gone to a birthday party and Sammy was having his nap, Sarah seduced him.

It was unexpected. There was not much opportunity lately, with the kids around all the time, and especially since James had been sleeping in the spare room. This was supposed to be a temporary arrangement. Sarah had complained that he was restless in the night, snoring loudly and disturbing her, though he had not been aware of it himself. At first it had just been the odd night – she would wake him up and ask him to go into the other room. Then she suggested he go to bed in there to start with, just for a few nights, to save them both the disruption. That had been weeks ago. Now the Bell's had transformed his face and on top of this he had embarrassed them in front of their friends.

Nevertheless, after lunch he had gone up to the spare room for a nap himself, and ten minutes later, just as he was dozing off, Sarah came in and stood in the doorway. She was silent at first, and unsmiling, and James assumed she was getting ready to have a go at him for his behaviour the night before.

'I'm sorry,' James began, 'I was out of order. But, you know... the dog.'

Sarah didn't reply but walked over to the bed and lay down next to him. She propped her head up on one hand, facing towards him. She put her other hand between his legs.

'Do you remember when we used to screw in the afternoons?' she said.

There was no further preamble. The sex was good: urgent and surprisingly long. Sarah was on top of him, as he preferred it – doing all the work, she used to say – her back arched and her breasts raised up. She seemed unusually aroused, James thought, gripping him fiercely, but perhaps he had just forgotten what it was like. They did not kiss, a concession to his half-frozen mouth, he supposed, but, if anything, this restraint only added to the charged mood. After a few minutes Sarah came to a shuddering climax – it was rare that she would finish before him – and then went down on him until he came too. As she did so he heard himself making peculiar little grunts, the effect of his impeded mouth.

They lay in silence for a minute or two, breathing heavily.

'You're not put off, then?' said James.

Sarah looked at him.

'My face…' he said.

'Should I be?'

James could feel his erection returning and he wondered, to his own surprise, whether they might start again. Just as this idea was taking hold in his mind, however, Sarah rolled over and got out of bed.

'I'm late to get Laura,' she said.

Once Sarah had gone, James tried again for his nap, but the moment had passed so after a few minutes he got up and went for a shower.

He did remember when they used to screw in the afternoons. Before the kids, at weekends, or on the rare occasion during the week when neither of them was at work. This was the ultimate decadence, going to bed in the middle of the day for the sole purpose of sex. He remembered the sweet sense of transgression, of knowing that while the rest of the world went about the humdrum and deferred gratification of their daily lives – perhaps sitting on a bus or train or in the car or, more than likely, in a meeting or in front of a computer screen in an office – they were engaged in something essential and elemental. It was a statement, somehow, of pure life. Throughout the first year or two they were together, they had been rampant, took every opportunity and had been proud of it. Even when they had sex right before going to sleep, James used to wake up in the middle of the night with an erection and begin to move against her. Wordlessly and still half-asleep they would do it again. Sometimes, in the mornings, James did not even remember these encounters – The Midnight Rapist, Sarah called them – until she reminded him.

All this seemed a long time ago. Over the years their sex life had suffered in the normal way. From exhaustion, the stresses of work and the kids, and a certain amount of boredom too, James supposed. For a while they had talked about it and said they must try harder, but increasingly it had just become a subject to be avoided out of embarrassment. Before today he couldn't quite remember the last time it had happened – certainly before his night-time restlessness had exiled him to the spare room.

He was out of the shower now and standing in front of the full-length mirror in the bedroom. He wasn't in bad shape, he thought. If anything, he looked better at forty than he had at twenty. The thin, runty, narrow-shouldered, late-to-develop body he had been mildly ashamed of had finally come into its own. Now, most of the other men he knew of his age had got fat or were struggling not to, while he stayed lean and sharp-edged without really exercising or worrying about what he ate. There was also his hair – which others were losing or had lost – of which he had always been secretly, excessively proud. It was dark and thick, with a slight curl that came out when it was longer and which he liked to think, half-seriously, was the expression of some inner vigour or vitality. He was sure women looked at him now in a way they rarely had when he was younger.

The children had given him a strange sort of sexual confidence, too. They were incontrovertible evidence of his virility, his evolutionary advantage. This was pretty absurd, he knew, but he suspected other men felt the same way. It made him remember the surge of confidence he had got in the days after sleeping with someone new – with Sarah and the relatively small number of women before her – when afterwards he would walk down the street and see the world in a different way, feeling that any of these women walking towards him were potential sexual partners.

James was adrift in his thoughts when he heard Sammy starting to stir in his room. He turned away from the mirror and began to get dressed.

7

THE CONSULTANT AT THE HOSPITAL HAD SAID IT could take up to three weeks before James's face began to show any sign of improvement and that, initially, it could even get a little worse. He resolved to cope with this as well as he could in the meantime, to bear it with some kind of dignity.

The most difficult thing was not being at work. It was strange to think how attached to his job he had become. James had fallen into it more or less by accident at the tail end of his twenties and drifted along for several years, wondering what else he might do for the long term. Then, when they found out Sarah was pregnant with Laura, he had, without making any conscious decision, begun to take it more seriously. In doing so he discovered a flair and appreciation for the work that he had previously not suspected. At an appraisal around this time, Deborah, his manager, told him that clients liked working with him. 'You win people over, James,' she said, 'you know how to read a situation. Not everyone has that.' All this coincided with the firm beginning a rapid expansion and he had, so to speak, ridden the wave. He had been given several quick promotions, the first of which had enabled them to buy the house in New Glades and take on a bigger mortgage.

For the last six months he had been leading a project at a law firm, an old family business with a complicated range of management and personnel problems. James's remit had been broad, to assess and implement the changes need to modernise the company and make it more competitive. Some of this was technological – they barely had a working computer system – and although James was not strictly a tech person he understood the fundamentals. His real talent, though, was for strategic thinking, for understanding the changes needed to systems and processes, for seeing the larger picture. 'Troubleshooting' was how he usually described his work to anyone who asked, 'glorified troubleshooting'. This was the biggest project of his career so far, and it had, at times, been very challenging. The staff had been resistant to his ideas, though this was to some degree inevitable. A minority had been actively uncooperative, even openly hostile, believing it was all simply a smokescreen for redundancies, but James had persevered and finally things had started to fall into place.

Just before Christmas, when the school and nursery terms had ended but James was still at work, Sarah had brought the kids to meet him for lunch. Somehow they had never got around to doing this before and he was surprised at how excited – almost jumpy – he was all morning at the prospect, at showing his colleagues to his children and his children to his colleagues. He had made a big fuss of them at reception, surprising Sarah by giving her a hug as well as the children. He had given them a brief tour of the building. They had relocated there recently after taking on more staff, a vast warehouse that had once stored the giant rolls of paper used by newspaper printing presses and now reinvented as a modern office building for a number of companies broadly similar to James's own. As they went round, James had introduced them elaborately to people he barely knew and had laughed too hard at things that were not really jokes.

In the end, the visit was rather anti-climactic. He took them up to his own office at the top of the building, and his desk by the window. He showed Laura and Sammy how far you could see, the landmarks around the city, the smallness of the cars and people moving around on the street below. He pointed out a dark green smudge in the distance that he told the children was their own woods, though in reality this was unlikely. They were not particularly impressed. Laura was annoyed because she had wanted to spend the day at a friend's house and Sammy was hungry and needed a nap. A couple of James's colleagues stopped to say hello but quickly made excuses about how busy they were and hurried on. When James sat Sammy in his office chair and spun it too fast, he began to cry bitterly and after only a few minutes they hurried out of the building to get some food.

When it became clear that he would be off for more than a few days, James briefed Deborah over the phone. She had been relaxed about it, more relaxed than James felt he would be if the situation were reversed. He offered to work from home, answering emails and going over documents, but she had refused. 'If you're sick, you're sick,' she said. 'This isn't the kind of job you can do at a distance.' This was decent of her, of course, but he had felt himself bristle at her choice of words. He had wanted to correct her, to say, 'I'm not sick, it's just a problem with my face.' In the event, he was glad he did not. The distinction seemed important to James, but it would only have made him sound difficult, pedantic. And anyway, as far as his office was concerned, the result was the same – he was not there. 'Concentrate on getting well, James,' Deborah went on. 'Let us worry about things here.' She was right. He was a good employee and before this hadn't had an unscheduled day off in two years. It was frustrating, but work and the project would survive without him for a while and he without it. It was important to have some perspective about that.

James had often thought, over the last six years of parenthood and long hours at the office, about the sorts of things he would do if he had the time – the books he would read, the old friends he would catch up with, the new language or musical instrument he would learn. The ordinary fantasies of a person his age with a demanding job and young children, he knew, but it would be something just to be able to sit with a cup of coffee and a newspaper at the kitchen table in the morning, with nowhere he needed to be and no one waiting for him to do something. Well, here was an opportunity of sorts, an enforced lay-off, the kids out of the house for the better part of the day, if not exactly how he had anticipated it.

Before New Glades, they had lived for nearly ten years in a flat on the ninth floor of a tower block in the inner city, at the corner of two busy roads. Police, ambulance and fire-engine sirens went off continually and because of some trick of the acoustics, the vehicles sounded almost as if they were driving through the middle of their tiny living room. At night, kids or drunks pressed the door buzzer on the street, just for the hell of it, and woke the baby. 'Super-urban' was how James often described it after they moved away. Even when you were in the flat alone you had the sense of the city, the concrete, the cars, the people, the bad air pressing in all around you.

New Glades, of course, was different. If he stood at an upstairs window and concentrated he could, just about, pick up the hum of traffic on the main road, muted almost to nothing by the woods that surrounded the estate on three sides. Once a week, on Tuesday afternoons, there was the sound of the communal lawns being mown or the hedges being clipped, and on Thursdays the bin men came. If he heard a car on the road outside, James usually went to the window to look. The phone rang rarely, and if it did it was almost always Sarah. His mobile had no reception in the house – people said the trees blocked the signal – and they had never got round to giving out the landline number.

Gradually, however, as the days went past, James tuned into two other, more or less constant, sounds. The first was of Kit at work on his house, the dull but relentless industry of hammering, sawing, sanding and drilling. The other was the song, if that was the right word, of the parakeets. There were ten or fifteen of them in the flock that flew in and out of the cherry tree, scarlet-beaked, green-bodied, shading to blue and yellow and gold in the wings and tail feathers. They were never far away, patrolling the border where the woods and the estate met. There were other birds too, of course – sparrows, blue tits, blackbirds, robins, crows and magpies – though James did not know which song belonged to which bird. The parakeets', though, could not be mistaken. It peaked at dawn and again at dusk, a frenzy of atonal shrieking and squawking, and it was hard to believe he had barely been aware of it before. When James looked them up online he discovered that there were flocks of them all over the city, breeding fast, eating everything and pushing out the native species. Nevertheless, when he caught sight of them through the window or when he stepped outside the front door, their non-native colours brash against the brilliant white of the cherry blossoms that had already begun to bloom, as if the tree were heavy with some alien fruit, it was not hard to forgive them for this clamour.

Each morning, once Sarah and the children had gone, James finished his breakfast – it was still taking him much longer than everyone else to eat – cleared up the kitchen and put a load of washing on. Then, at around ten o'clock, he put on his boots and jacket, went down the steps, crossed the road and opened the gate in the laurel

47

hedge. He took arbitrary zigzagging routes through the woods, allowing himself to be led by whim and curiosity. There were always new ways to be found by pushing aside a branch or climbing over a fallen trunk. Some of the massive oaks, James had read, were centuries old, the remainder of a vast forest that had once stretched for miles over what was now the city, a place where aristocrats had come to hunt boar and deer. This was all that was left, perhaps twenty-five acres, bordered on the northern side by a golf course, on the east by allotments, on the west by a busy A-road and on the south by New Glades itself, an oasis and an anomaly amid the encroaching city. It was not much, but it was big enough to get lost in, at least for a while.

It was spring and there were new things every day. The rhododendron flowers in a spray down the front of the train tunnel, patches of hornbeam coming into leaf. The woodpeckers continued their work and occasionally, if he stood patiently and listened, he was able to spot one high up in the trees. From time to time mists of pollen swept across the path in front of him, catching the light. In this way, the walks were restorative, invigorating, and he was often out of the house for as much as an hour. It seemed the ideal way to counteract the lethargy that had crept in during the first week of the palsy and that threatened to overtake him whenever he was in the house. Simple observation of the vivid material world took him out of himself, absorbed him in something else. He often found, when he got back home, that for the duration of his walk he had not thought of his palsy at all.

Then, towards the end of his third week off work, two things happened in quick succession which rather threw him.

8

THE FIRST THING HAPPENED ON A FRIDAY MORNING.
James had gone out early, before ten, and had been
walking for nearly an hour along a route that had taken
him up among the ruined houses and then down along
the path of a stream to the high spiked metal fence of the
golf course. He had traced the path of the fence around
the northern perimeter of the woods, listening for the
crack of balls being hit, and then cut east by the side of
the allotments. It was time to head home, and he pulled
back a low branch that hung in front of him and stepped
onto the wide, well-trodden track that bisected the
woods and went down to the station. A few metres away,
coming towards him, was a runner. It was the serious
kind: grim-faced, head to toe in fluorescent Lycra, with
headband and wraparound sunglasses, headphones in
and another gadget, perhaps a heart monitor, strapped
to his arm. They were a pretty common sight around

the neighbourhood and in the woods themselves.

James's appearance on the path seemed to surprise him and throw him off his stride. He veered abruptly to the right and tripped on a small tree stump, and his momentum took him heavily and awkwardly into the undergrowth.

James rushed over. 'Are you okay?' he asked.

The man was already on his feet. He had a ragged-looking scratch – more than that, a gash – on his right cheek and a piece of skin was flapping off. It was bleeding profusely, running down his face and dripping onto his top.

He was adjusting the headphones in his ears. He seemed unaware of his injury, the blood, or unwilling to acknowledge it. He didn't look at James.

'I didn't see you,' the runner said.

He looked at his watch, took two steps and was off, running again.

'You're hurt!' called out James, but the runner gave no sign of having heard. 'I'm sorry,' James shouted, as loudly as his mouth would allow. The man was twenty yards away now, getting smaller. Then the path twisted, and abruptly he was out of sight altogether.

At home later that evening, when the kids had gone to bed, he described what had happened to Sarah and she had laughed.

'What's funny?' asked James.

'It's just the thought of you skulking around in the woods and then jumping out at someone.'

'I wasn't skulking around.'

'Well, what were you doing in there?'

'Oh, just – walking,' James said. Then, 'There was quite a lot of blood.'

'You said. I'm sure he'll live.'

'I suppose so,' said James, but when he went to bed he still couldn't get the sight of the man's face out of his mind, the gash, the flap of skin and the blood, the surprising amount of it.

The following day, Saturday, it was bright again, and warm, the warmest day of the year so far. A week before, Sammy, who had been shuffling along on his bottom for months, had stood up and started walking and so now Sarah had taken him to buy his first proper shoes. Laura was out on the grassy verge between the road and the laurel hedge that bordered the wood. She liked to wander up and down, inspecting the ground, looking for the green and yellow feathers of the parakeets. She said she was going to make them into a headdress, like ones she had seen in pictures of Native Americans.

James sat in the deckchair that they kept on the front porch all year round, reading the newspaper. It was his favourite spot around the house, ten steps above road level, partly shaded by the cherry tree, with a view over the woods and on to the city, the same view that had mirrored his elation the morning of Sammy's birth.

After a few minutes his eye became too sore to read and he put the paper down and lay back in the chair. He closed his right eye and placed the palm of his hand over his left. He could hear the buzz of insects, and the woodpeckers again, a satisfying, industrious noise that made him feel paradoxically relaxed, as well as the gentle, indecipherable murmur of Laura chattering to herself as she walked up and down the verge. The sun warmed his face and a drifting, disembodied feeling began to over-take him. Sarah had once told him that ten minutes of the sun on your face a day gave you all the vitamin D you needed and lifted your mood – or something like that. In the same way, it seemed possible that the sun's benev-olent rays might have the power to relax and unfreeze his face, to nourish it back into life.

'I've got something,' Laura called out. 'Daddy, I've got something. What is it?'

James opened his eyes and looked over to where she was standing on the verge, a little bit obscured by the knotty, twisting trunk of the cherry tree, something dangling from her left hand.

'What is it, Daddy?'

The sun was in his eyes.

'I can't see from here, sweetheart.'

'I'm coming.'

She turned and started to cross the road. He watched her come, taking careful steps, her face fixed in concentration as if she were carrying a delicate piece of porcelain or china, something precious and easily smashed. She was six now, nearly seven – it was hard to believe. She had grown much taller and thinner in the last few months, revealing long, lean limbs. Sarah had taken her for a new, shorter haircut, with a fringe that she pushed or blew out of her eyes, and this too made her seem older. Her eyes were large, brown, very round and somehow soulful, a quality that was often caught in photos. People often told him how pretty she was and this pleased James more than he thought it really should.

She was quiet but not shy, a little serious perhaps, and had a kind of serene self-possession that already made people – adults and children – want to be friends with her, and that would later, it seemed to James, make people fall in love with her. When she was small it had been easy. If she was happy, she laughed or smiled. If she cried then she was hungry or tired or needed her nappy changed. Increasingly, however, and particularly since she had started school, she was becoming an enigma to him. She knew and said things that surprised him, had her own unguessable thoughts and moods, things she did and didn't want to talk about, levels of complexity he could know nothing about. This seemed in some obscure way unreasonable. He had been there the day of her birth and every day since, all the important moments, and yet now his belief that he knew more about her, understood her better, than she did herself was beginning to have to give way. No doubt it was all completely normal and inevitable for Laura to change the way she was, for him to feel the way he did about it. He supposed he had just not expected it to happen so soon.

She was coming up the steps to the porch now, treading over some of the cherry blossom that had already fallen or been knocked from the tree, and she looked up at him and gave a tentative, almost sly smile. The sun had dipped behind a cloud and the thing she was holding was coming into focus. It was perhaps ten centimetres long, translucent but tinted red, knotted at the top just above where his daughter's little fist was gripping it, a nipple shaped protuberance at the bottom. Visible inside the nipple was an opaque, not-quite-white fluid, and as Laura climbed the steps the whole thing swung lazily from side to side, describing an unmistakably obscene arc through the blue air.

9

HALF AN HOUR LATER, JAMES WAS STANDING IN the shower. He had washed himself twice thoroughly, and shampooed his hair – unnecessarily, he knew – and was now leaning against the tiles, letting the water stream over his face and down his body.

In retrospect, the moments following his realisation of what Laura had in her hand seemed to occur in melodramatic, almost comical slow motion. The mangled cry of warning from his half-frozen mouth, launching himself out of the deckchair and grabbing his daughter's wrist so hard that she screamed and began to cry, the sun simultaneously bursting from behind the cloud and bathing them in warmth.

Laura had dropped the condom and James had half led, half pulled her into the house, where she continued to cry. He hugged her shaking, furious body.

'You hurt me, Daddy!' she wailed. 'You hurt me!'

'I'm sorry, darling,' he said, aware that he was shaking himself. 'It's just – some things you shouldn't touch, if you don't know what they are.'

He held her for a little longer while her crying subsided. Then he carried her over to the kitchen sink and washed her hands. There was a red mark on her wrist from where his hand had been. He got her a drink and a biscuit and put on the television.

'You are naughty, Daddy,' she said, but her tone was calm now, matter-of-fact, and she was staring at the TV.

James went back out to the porch. His blood was still pumping and he sat down on the wall to take some breaths and try and reason with himself. His daughter was right. The scene had been unnecessary. He saw that he had made the incident entirely worse than it had needed to be. He had upset Laura – a child who was not easily upset – and made her feel that she had done something wrong, that something, in some way, was her fault. As unpleasant and unhygienic as it was, she could not come to any harm by touching the condom. It was not a live grenade or a venomous snake she was holding, or even a rusty nail or a piece of glass. As it was, it was he who had ended up, inadvertently, hurting her. Looking at it now, lying flat and twisted on the paving stone, a wilted piece of garishly coloured, mass-produced latex, bathetic evidence of someone's fleeting pleasure, he felt extremely foolish.

However, there was still the question of where to dispose of it. After several minutes he went back inside and got one of the small green bags they used to put Sammy's soiled nappies in. He knelt down over the condom and, with his hand inside the bag, closed his fingers around it, as he had seen dog owners do when picking up their animals' excrement. Then he drew the bag up around it and tied a knot with the handles. There was no question of having it in the house, however well wrapped up, so he carried the bag down the steps to the bins in the front garden. Even this did not feel quite sufficient. It was somehow still too close to the house – he would think of it sitting there, and the bins were not due to be collected for nearly a week. For a few moments he toyed with the idea of dropping it in a neighbour's bin – they wouldn't know it was there and it wouldn't trouble them – but, apart from anything else, he might be seen and it would be a hard one to explain. Then, without realising he was about to do it, like a reflex kicking in, James drew back his arm and flung the bag high in the air, over the road, over the laurel bushes and into the woods themselves. He did not hear it land.

*

James had replayed all this in his mind as he stood in the shower. The wash had made him feel better, calmer and more clear-headed, but when he finally stepped out onto the shower mat and used a towel to wipe condensation from the bathroom mirror, he received his second shock of the day. This, it seemed, was what had really been waiting for him, hovering just out of view.

A couple of weeks before, he had stood in front of the same mirror after sex with Sarah, and – quite absurdly, it seemed now – admired what he saw. He had managed then, and in general ever since the first morning in the bathroom, and although he had been in front of the mirror several times every day to shave and clean his teeth – to somehow fail or refuse to see what was in front of him. It was a form of self-preservation, he supposed. But it hit him now, forcefully, all over again, the discord between left and right, the grotesqueness of something familiar pulled violently out of shape. This, of course, was the stricken, agonised face that had loomed out from among the trees and sent the runner careering off the path and into the undergrowth.

And then, looking closer, there was his left eye, straining in its socket. The pupil was very large, almost engorged, the yellowing cornea red-rimmed and mapped with blood vessels. It stared unblinkingly back at him, as if from some slightly other place. Again, there was the hint of accusation and judgement – now with some justification, James reflected – for having shouted and been rough with his daughter, for having been negligent in letting her pick up the condom in the first place, for something more complicated and less articulable altogether. He had to remind himself that it was his own eye he was looking at and that was looking at him, but this was hardly reassuring.

Part Two

I

THREE TIMES A DAY, WHEN HE WOKE UP, AFTER
lunch and after dinner, James stood in front of the bathroom mirror and attempted the exercises the consultant
had given him: puckering his lips, raising his eyebrows,
wrinkling his forehead and his nose. As he was doing
them he tried to picture the nerve endings rebuilding,
reconnecting, coming alive again, the way Sarah had
described it to Laura on the first day, as if this positive visualisation and force of will might somehow help
the process. He applied himself conscientiously, but
noticed no difference. The left-hand side of his lips,
his forehead, his left nostril and his eyebrow remained
resolutely frozen. And even these five-minute sessions
– this was all the consultant had recommended – left
him feeling utterly depleted, as if in the effort to move
his face he had been pushing at some great and immov-
able weight. Sometimes, afterwards, he lay down on

the spare-room bed and fell immediately into a doze.

He took the steroids, a little blue pill, with his dinner every night, and used the eye drops. He started wearing a patch, too. Sarah had got it for him at the beginning but he had resisted putting it on, feeling it would make him look a little ridiculous, piratical, more conspicuous rather than less. Now, on balance, he felt it was worth it. It was a little uncomfortable and he kept having to adjust the position, but the eye itself was less sore. This way there was no chance of him catching sight of it in the mirror or reflected in a window or on the computer screen, this unsettling, inflamed presence, and – just as importantly, it seemed – other people were protected from the sight of it, too.

But it had now been nearly six weeks since the palsy had struck, surely well past the 'few weeks' the GP had said it might take to begin the recovery, and he could not help brooding on it. When he was alone in the house, barely occupied, he could not avoid it. It was the context for everything in his narrowed life. How he ate, how he talked, where he could go and what he could do, all thoughts of the day-to-day and the immediate future, nothing could be considered without it. For a few minutes at a time he might lose himself in something else, perhaps when he was reading the newspaper online or listening to the radio, but then something would remind him, the feel of his face when he scratched his nose – strange, alien – or just the realisation of where he was, at home, in the middle of the day, in the middle of the week.

It had all started to look horribly open-ended. 'Almost definitely,' the GP had said when James asked if it would get better. She had meant to reassure him, but now her statement began to stand for the opposite outcome. 'Only a small percentage do not return to more or less normal.' That small percentage had to be made up of individuals, individuals like himself, perhaps. And anyway, what did 'more or less normal' mean? How normal was that? Was this the best he could hope for?

Meanwhile, time weighed heavily on him. He had not taken up a musical instrument or started to learn a new language. He could just about manage to read the news but did not have the concentration span for anything longer. The last thing he wanted to do was contact old friends. As she had promised on the first day, Sarah had given him a list of things that needed doing – pictures that needed hanging, paintwork to be touched up, small jobs in the garden – but somehow he had made little headway with these either.

From time to time James contemplated getting off the estate altogether for a morning or an afternoon. Perhaps an expedition to the outside world was just what he needed – to see normal life going on would do him good, keep him human. But each time he thought about it, the reasons against quickly piled up. He could not drive because of his eye, and anyway Sarah had the car. It was a good walk to a bus stop that could then take him somewhere else. He imagined the struggle he would have to express himself to a bus driver or someone in a shop, the looks he might get, the pity. But more than any of this, he could not really think where to go – to an art gallery, to a café, to sit alone in a cinema in the middle of the day? One morning he walked to the station, taking his old route through the woods, and stood on the platform while three trains came and went.

One of the things James missed most was being out of the house all day and then coming home again. From time to time, throughout the winter, and the one before, when he approached the house along the road in the evening, he had played a game with himself. He climbed the steps quietly and instead of going straight in, he lingered by the front window and looked through the blinds at Sarah and Laura and Sammy, perhaps watching television or eating dinner. And as he stood there in the dark he liked to imagine that he did not know these people, that he was a stranger staring in on someone else's life, somewhere warm, brightly lit and comfortable, envying their good luck. Then, when he was lost in this daydream, one of the children would notice him and shout 'Daddy's home!' or wave, and he would smile and take out his keys.

Now, the situation was reversed. He was at home, waiting for Sarah and the kids. He looked forward to them getting back in the late afternoon, but when they did, the sudden change of pace was difficult, the noise and chaos, and he was often grumpy and short-tempered. On the worst days he went up to the spare room for a few minutes to escape them and calm himself down. Sarah did not complain about this or indeed about anything else. She was dropping the kids off and picking them up as usual, doing the shopping, going to work and then coming home and taking care of things there, dealing with the full strain of family life. James, on the other hand, was idle, more or less useless, contributing almost nothing to what had previously been a joint effort. Sarah did not even complain about his failure to do the few small jobs she had given him, and this had the effect of making him feel more guilty rather than less.

This pragmatism and lack of drama had always been one of the things he had appreciated about Sarah most, but he began to feel, perversely, that he would be happier if she were not coping so well. It made him wonder if she pined for their normal old life the way he did.

'It's amazing what we can get used to,' the doctor had said.

One Saturday evening, when he had been complaining of his restlessness and frustration, Sarah said, 'James, you need a hobby.'

'A hobby?'

'Yes. Like Greg and his butchery. Not that, but something like it. Probably all men need a hobby.'

They were eating dinner, the whole family together around the kitchen table, Sammy in his high chair, and, after a short pause, during which he did not know what he was going to do, James threw down his cutlery and stood up.

'A fucking hobby!' he shouted, feeling the colour rise in the right-hand side of his face. Laura and Sammy looked up from their food, startled and confused. James turned and stamped his way furiously upstairs.

There had been no more seductions or sex in the afternoon, or at any other time, but he had not felt able to raise this with Sarah or even to refer to that occasion. He was still in the spare room and this seemed, also without discussion, to have become more than a temporary arrangement. Laura had begun to refer to it as 'Daddy's room' and after a while James stopped correcting her. He got up later in the mornings, after the others had gone, and in the evening Sarah went to bed early.

And there was something else. James had not told Sarah about the incident with the condom. He had not planned it that way, but when she had come in that afternoon she was in a good mood. Sammy had toddled up and down the living room in his new shoes, laughing, and it had not seemed like the right moment. Then, in the evening, after the kids were in bed, he had almost told her but then, guiltily, decided not to. There was something unsavoury about it all that he did not want to repeat or re-live. He was also, he supposed, ashamed of the way he had dealt with it, making Laura cry and then throwing the condom into the woods. Sarah would, rightly, think him ridiculous. And as each day went by without his mentioning it, it seemed harder to bring up. He expected that Laura would tell Sarah about it soon enough, and that he would have to deal with it then, but apparently she did not. He tried once to talk to Laura about it himself.

'You know that thing you found out on the grass?' he said one evening when he found himself alone with her in the kitchen.

She looked thoughtful and then, after a few seconds, said, 'Daddy, you know when one of your teeth falls out at school? They give you a little bag to put it in so you can take it home.'

'Yes, but darling...' he said to her, but trailed off

when he saw that she was not listening. He had not tried again after that. She had not raised it with him either, to ask what it was she had found on the verge and carried up the steps, or why he had reacted the way he had. This seemed strange but you could never predict the things that would preoccupy or make an impression on children. Still, it all hung over him, the inadvertent deceit and the seeming inevitability that it would come out at some point and reflect badly on him.

2

'THE INSTALLATION OF CCTV CAMERAS AT KEY points around the estate,' said William, 'offers a number of benefits. The first is obvious. Our night-time visitors can be monitored, cars identified, and the details passed to the police to follow up. In addition, it would discourage other undesirables: fly-tippers, non-residents who use the estate as a car park for visiting the woods and anyone else who has no good reason to be here.'

The committee was meeting at Kit's house for the first time. The place was identical in dimensions and layout to James's own house but immaculately presented and with sure signs of childlessness – a long glass coffee table, white carpets, various delicate-looking ornaments and pictures displayed on low shelves. Kit had just finished the redecoration of the living room, James overheard him say to another committee member, and it smelt strongly of paint and newly unwrapped furniture. It was also the first meeting since James's palsy had appeared and so far it had been something of a struggle. 'Apologies for my face,' he had said as soon he called the meeting to order, 'a temporary problem,' and then moved briskly on. But he was not used to talking so much, and the effort of it – and of trying to make his words come out clearly – was tiring.

The CCTV cameras had not even been on the agenda. The meeting was supposed to have been focused on arrangements for the New Glades summer party in June, a relatively straightforward dividing-up of jobs among the committee members. This was an event James himself enjoyed and which he had come to see as the embodiment of the best qualities – communal, social – of the estate. However, William had given his neighbour-hood watch report, which included four more instances of The Anti-Social Behaviour, one couple discovered in flagrante in the middle of the day, and they had been sidetracked.

Perhaps it was to do with not having been at work, where he ran meetings all the time and thrived on it, or in the outside world much at all for the last month, but to be the centre of attention here was a little unnerving and James did not feel his usual confidence. Despite his early effort to neutralise any awkwardness, he was conscious of the state of his face and what the other members of the committee might be making of it. There was another thing, a mistake that seemed obvious to him now. In the past he had arrived at these meetings straight from work, in his suit and no doubt with the air of the office still about him. This evening he had not bothered to change out of the clothes he wore to walk in the woods, an old jumper and jeans that he now noticed were flecked with mud. Over the last couple of weeks he had given up shaving, too. The slackness of the skin on the left-hand side of his face, and the lack of sensation there, made it awkward – he had cut himself several times – and anyway, it hardly seemed necessary at the moment. Now, as well as the eye patch, he had a scraggy, faintly gingerish beard, which did at least conceal some of his disfigured face. These were the small things that could drain power from you and he sensed a diminishing in his authority over the committee, a resistance to his attempts to control and steer the meeting. Already the discussion about the cameras had gained too much momentum.

'This... proposal,' said James, trying hard to conceal his exasperation, 'has been considered, and then rejected, on a number of occasions by earlier incarnations of this committee on logistical, financial and, you might say, philosophical grounds. It is not something I would propose to revisit here.' He was very aware of the sound of his own voice, strained and feeble, pompous and pedantic, almost comically so.

'But I am unclear,' said Vanessa, patting down the folds of the tie-dye dress she was wearing, 'what you propose to do instead? The police say they will send more patrols but we know this won't happen or won't make any difference. And we know from past experience that the problem will only get worse as the weather warms up. The sap is rising, I'm afraid. There will only be more of this... dogging.'

'Ah, no, this is not dogging,' said James, glad to be able to make a point of fact. 'Dogging is when people gather to watch other people having sex in cars, or other public places for that matter. As far as I know,' he said, attempting a smile, 'that is not happening here.'

He had hoped that this might yield some laughter from around the room and get the meeting on his side, but apparently it did not. Vanessa was looking sourly at him.

'Anyway,' he went on hurriedly, 'we don't need to dwell on terminology. I think we can all agree that it is undesirable. But with respect to the cameras, I think we have to ask ourselves what sort of place it is that we want to live in.'

The four instances recorded by William in his report did not include Laura finding the condom on the verge by the woods. It was a little different, James told himself. Neither he nor – God forbid – Laura had witnessed anyone having sex in a car and he had no way of being sure where it had come from. On the one hand it seemed almost too trivial to mention, and, on the other, too unsavoury. In the same way that he had been reluctant to share it with Sarah, he did not want to tell this unpleasant story of which his daughter was the protagonist and victim. Not to mention that he was ashamed at the way he had dealt with it. Anyway, he could hardly tell the committee when he had not told his wife. More than likely someone would then mention it to her. On top of all this, given the apparently febrile mood of the meeting, the last thing he wanted to do was provide a story that would further vindicate their desire for action.

'Personally, I want to live in a place where I won't find people shagging on my doorstep,' said Kit.

Kit had been moving around the room discreetly, getting the rest of the committee drinks and passing round trays of fussy-looking snacks that he had prepared himself, but was now sitting cross-legged on the floor – barefoot, James noticed. 'With all due respect to our chair,' he went on, using James's title unnecessarily and, James thought, with a note of condescension, 'the fact that these cameras have been mooted before doesn't seem to me an argument for not considering them now.

Quite the opposite, in fact. It shows that this is a problem that won't go away and needs fixing. This is private land and it is our prerogative to choose who comes onto it.'

'That is all very well,' said James, 'but even if we were to agree it among ourselves, we would encounter the usual obstacles and bureaucracy...'

'In fact,' Kit interrupted, 'I have spoken to the trust and they are very receptive to residents' concerns about security. They have suggested we submit a proposal to them and they will consider it favourably as well as whether they can subsidise the cost.'

James was startled. One of the committee's principal functions was to represent the views of all residents to the trust in the person of the chair. However, he sensed that this was not the moment at which to make a point about formal procedures. Kit was still sitting on the floor, ostentatiously it seemed to James, as there were several free chairs. It was as if, by sitting at James's feet, he was expressing some kind of deference to his position, but the effect, as Kit surely knew, was the opposite.

'Well, that's as may be,' James said, gathering himself, 'but I would return to my earlier point. These things are symbolic. Do we really want our every move recorded on camera – our children, too?' Here he made sure to sweep his eyes – his eye – around the whole group. 'To send the message to visitors that they are essentially unwelcome here? And where would it stop? Should we have a fence, or even a wall, patrolled by dogs or armed guards?'

'Now you are being hysterical,' said Kit.

'I am being hysterical? Me?'

No one spoke, and as he looked around at the rest of the committee he felt a quiver in the atmosphere of the room. They were looking at him more carefully now, a palpable change in the quality of their attention, and James was relieved that he was finally getting his point across.

He was about to go on when William said, 'James, you are crying.'

'Excuse me?'

'You seem to be crying.'

At that moment, James looked down and watched a large tear splash heavily onto the notes in front of him. He saw that the ink was smeared from ones that had already fallen. He put his hand to his face, the left-hand side, and his beard was quite damp. He touched the other side and it was dry.

William handed him a tissue. James lifted up his eye patch and the pool of tears that had collected underneath it streamed down his face.

'Don't worry,' he said, 'I know what this is. I'm fine, it's just my – my eye.' He dabbed the tissue on his eye and then held it there. 'Okay. What else, then? What are we doing about music for the party this year?'

James tried to go on but the tears kept coming. The tissue was already soaked through.

'Or the booze. Who wants to take care of that?'

No one spoke. James looked around the room. Several of the committee members looked away, others fidgeted with their pens or phones. He saw that they were embarrassed.

'James,' said Vanessa, 'perhaps we should adjourn for this evening.'

James looked around the room again.

'Yes, okay,' he said. 'Perhaps that is sensible.'

He collected up his notes and put them in his bag. It seemed to take forever and still no one spoke. Then he pushed back his chair, and went out.

3

THE NEXT MORNING, JAMES WENT TO SEE THE doctor again.

It was not really because of what had happened at the meeting. By the time he had got home, a few doors down, the tears had stopped. He had not even mentioned it to Sarah. She was in bed when he got back and he had only seen her briefly in the morning before she rushed out with the children. Anyway, he knew what it was. He had read that this could happen to people with Bell's. Sometimes when the facial nerves regrew they made the wrong connections, causing tears to well up spontaneously. It even had a name, Crocodile Tears Syndrome. In fact, as soon as he had woken up he had sent an email to the committee, self-deprecatory in tone, apologising for 'making a scene', and suggesting that Kit and any other interested parties put together a formal proposal for the cameras that could be considered at the next meeting.

But certainly his face was no better than it had been at the beginning and the doctor had told him to come back if he needed to. Perhaps there was something else that could be done. Moreover, without another doctor's note, he was due back at work the following week. He tried to picture himself at his desk or in a meeting, and then the possibility of a scene like the one at the committee meeting but among his professional colleagues instead, or, even worse, trying to manage one of the delicate interactions with the staff at the law firm, the Q & As where he stood alone in front of a sceptical and belligerent audience. It was hard to see, at this point, how he would be ready for any of that.

It was Dr Moffat again. James gave her a summary of the last few weeks. He said that as far as he could tell there had been no real change in his condition and that he still had no movement or sensation in the left-hand side of his face. He outlined the difficulties he was having eating, drinking and talking, and described his daily routine – the walks in the woods, the naps – emphasising how conscientious he had been about taking the steroids and doing the exercises the consultant had given him. He finished by telling her what had happened with his eye the night before. While he was speaking she typed on the computer, punching the keys hard and fast with her two forefingers. Then she put on latex gloves and he took off the patch and lay on the examination table while she shined a light in his eyes and asked him to try and move his face in particular ways.

'Hmmm…' she said, 'hmmm…'

She looked, somehow, even bonier and greyer than the last time he had seen her.

'What do you think?' said James.

'Well,' she said, peeling off the gloves and dropping them in the bin. 'We do get cases that are, how shall I say, more… tenacious than others. Yours would seem to be one of them. But we are still early days as far as these things go. Let's keep an eye on it – as it were.' She smiled at him to acknowledge the pun.

She sat down and looked back at the computer screen.

'This crying. It just happened out of the blue you say?'

'It wasn't crying. There were tears but I wasn't crying. It's called Crocodile Tears Syndrome.'

'And how are you feeling in yourself? Any irritability? Problems concentrating?'

'No more than you would expect, I think.'

'Sure, sure,' said Moffat. 'What about mood swings, James?'

He was still lying on the examination table and she had her back to him while she continued to look at the computer.

'Look,' he said. 'Is there anything else I can do? Are there any other medications?'

'As a matter of fact, yes, there are. What I would like to do, based on what you have told me, is to prescribe something that will help you in a more general way.' She started to type again.

'I'm not sure...' began James.

'It's an anti-depressant medication but you really don't need to think of it that way. We prescribe them quite broadly these days.' She spun round in the chair and looked at him. There were very dark rings, like bruises, around her eyes. 'Living with any illness that has become...' She paused, and seemed to change her mind about what to say. '... that has gone on longer than we would like – well, that can be very challenging. It would just be a low dose. Even that can be very effective. You'd be amazed at what a little lift can do.'

'No thanks,' said James.

'Alternatively, we have a very good person here at the surgery who it might be helpful for you to talk to, to discuss how you're feeling. There's a bit of a waiting list but I can refer you.'

'No, I don't think that would help either.'

'Fine, fine. It's your choice, of course. The option is always there if you change your mind.'

She looked a little deflated but then her face lit up again.

'Look, I'm not an expert on the condition, but it seems to me that if you were crying – I mean, if there were tears coming out of your eye – then, as you say, the nerves must to some degree have regenerated, if not in quite the right way. Change, in my experience, is usually a good thing. Hold on to that thought, James! Did I tell you I had a boyfriend once who...'

'You did,' said James abruptly.

'Okay,' she said. 'Now hang on while I just write you this note for your work. I agree that it would be prema- ture to go back at this point. Let's give you another month and then see where we are.'

James continued to lie on the examination table, staring at the ceiling, and listened to the sound of her punching away at the keyboard for what seemed like a very long time.

Outside the surgery the sun was shining fiercely. James had taken a taxi to the appointment but in fact it was not too far to walk home, and the quickest way back was to cut through the woods. He went in through the gate on the north-eastern corner and began to walk up the wide lane that rose gently through the trees and then dropped down towards the station. He had been in there the day before, but overnight, it seemed, the woods had come into a new and florid lushness. The undergrowth, the grasses and nettles and bushes, had thickened, greened and leapt in height, spilling over onto the path. Vines as thick as his arm twisted, jungle-like, around the larger trees. This was some sort of cognitive illusion, James thought. These changes had been happening continuously, subtly, for weeks, even months. The vines had not grown overnight. It was happening now, too, but his senses, his brain, were not capable of registering them this way and instead he experienced it as abrupt, all at once. It was this way with the children, too. He saw them every day and yet one morning, out of the blue, he would see that they had grown an inch or that their face had taken on a new shape or expression. Change happened without you noticing it, and then you noticed it.

James didn't know how to feel about his appointment with Dr Moffat. He had been misunderstood, certainly, with regard to the anti-depressants. That was not helpful at all, but there was no point reading too much into it. He knew that it was the modern panacea, a GP's answer to any problem that evaded easy treatment. But he could not help dwelling on the word she had seemed to stop herself from using to describe his condition – chronic. Chronic meant long term, not temporary. Had he passed into that category now? Was that what she had typed into his notes? How long was long term?

Indefinite? It was well into May already and in another two months the children would be on summer holiday and at home all day. Then there was the trip to France with the Fullers to consider, too.

But it wouldn't do to get carried away. Dr Moffat had said it herself, it was early days for something like this. And perhaps she was also right about the significance of the tears, that it was a sign something was happening with the nerves at a fundamental level, even if it was not yet the right things. It did seem plausible.

Lost in thought, James realised that he was up among the foundations of the old houses. It was not the most direct way home. He knew the paths so well now that he could walk for long distances around the woods without paying conscious attention to where he was going, but this time he had led himself astray. Through the trees, twenty or thirty yards away, he could see the blue tarpaulin and below it the walls of the folly where the man was said to live. And there were clothes – black trousers, a white shirt and what looked like a suit jacket – hanging from the branches of a tree adjacent to it.

He turned off the path and walked through the undergrowth towards it. The three standing walls, up to around head height, were built of large blocks of grey stone, pockmarked with age and washed green with moss. The fourth, fallen, wall was laid out in a staged tumble of stones in front and James picked his way carefully around them. A moulded arch broke off in space, around three-quarters complete, and formed a partial entrance to the interior of the structure. Close up, as he was now for the first time, he was struck again by the strangeness of the place, a relic of another era's self-conscious attempt to create a relic, the layers of authentic and faked entropy.

The shirt and jacket hanging from the tree appeared clean, uncrumpled and in reasonable condition, hardly the outfit you would expect of someone who had been living rough for any amount of time. James stood on the threshold, under the arch, and looked in. It was no more than six feet square with a dirt floor. The light was dim, the tree cover and tarpaulin obscuring the brightness of the day outside. The air was cool, earthy, mildly fungal, not unpleasant. There was not much to see – what looked like a rolled-up sleeping bag tucked into a recess in the wall, a black duffle bag in one corner. A little hollow had been dug out in the centre and in it was the remains of a small fire, ringed by stones. The ground around it looked as if it had been made smooth, perhaps even recently swept.

It all seemed a little unreal, but it was not without precedent. James remembered something he had read soon after they had moved in, when he had taken a passing interest in the local history. For a period in the late seventeen hundreds, the woods had been home to a hermit known as 'Matthews the Hairyman'. A hunchback and herbalist, he had made his home in the hollow of a fallen tree. A much more feasible proposition in those days, James reflected, when the woods covered vast tracts of the land that was now paved over and built on, and not overrun by nature-starved city dwellers every weekend, but still. These days you would assume that someone living like this was homeless or destitute, someone without better options, but perhaps this was too simple. Maybe he had chosen to live there, for who knew what reasons, as presumably Matthews had more than two hundred years before. There was some kind of echo or symmetry there, perhaps.

Abruptly, the sensation he had felt when passing the camp before, of another human presence nearby, deliberately concealed perhaps, quite possibly watching, descended upon him. It was startling to find himself here, amid someone else's things, trespassing so flagrantly. He wondered what had possessed him to be so bold, so thoughtless. James stepped quickly out of the hollow and, with the lingering sense of someone's eyes on his back, hurried home.

4

LATER THAT AFTERNOON, WHEN HE WOKE UP from his nap, James called his office to let them know he had been signed off for another month.

In January, Deborah had told him he was on course to join the senior management team at the company within a year or two. She was expecting a promotion herself and wanted him to take over her current role. This was all before the palsy, of course. Now he could not help thinking about how his absence would be affecting these prospects, the project at the law firm that would already have become someone else's and for which they would get the credit.

From time to time, in the moments when he was feeling more positive, he thought that the answer would be simply to bite the bullet and go back to work, to force the issue. It would be difficult at first but the shock of it might revive him, instead of all the fretting and inactivity that surely only compounded his general lassitude. After all, it was this powerlessness over his situation that was really intolerable.

Work had put him under no pressure to return, and this was really a credit to them. At first he had called every Monday morning to update Deborah on his situation, but he had got the sense that this was unnecessarily conscientious. 'Just let us know when you are ready,' she had said, more than once. When he asked how things were going with the project she had chided him in a friendly way. 'That is not currently your concern,' she said, and then added, 'We are all thinking of you, James.' 'Really?' James had replied, taken aback. 'I mean, of course, thank you.'

He had got another doctor's note but no one had asked him for this, or in fact for the first one. Again, he was just being conscientious. Nevertheless, whenever he picked up the phone and heard it ring, he became intensely nervous, and this time, as every other time, he thought carefully about what he was going to say, almost as if he were preparing a lie.

In the event, he needn't have worried. The phone rang for some time and was then answered by someone, a man, whose voice he didn't recognise. Deborah was out of the office and this other man had picked up her phone, as James had done in the past.

'Can I leave a message?' said James. 'Can you say that James called?'

'Of course,' said the man. 'Can I take your surname, James?'

James could hear the hum of the office in the background, people talking, a printer clicking into action, other phones ringing. He tried again to picture himself there, as one of the people talking in the background perhaps, but the image refused to form.

'Orr,' said James. 'It's James Orr.'

'Can you spell that for me?'

James spelt out his name and then hung up. He opened the laptop and tried to log into his office emails. For weeks he had resisted doing this, on Deborah's instructions. Now his password seemed to have expired. On a whim he logged into his personal email account and sent a message to himself at work. Immediately an 'Out of Office' appeared. When he opened it, there was a message asking for any queries to be redirected to Deborah and giving her contact details.

It was strange to think of some unknown person logging in to – hacking, you might call it – his email account and setting up this brief, blunt message. They would have to have been given his password, a password that even he no longer knew. Probably it was a job given to some junior person in the office to sort out, perhaps the man he had just spoken to. James picked up the phone to call back, then hesitated and hung up again.

5

AT NIGHT, JAMES WAS HAVING TROUBLE SLEEPING.
He went to bed tired, but as soon as he switched off the
light, he began to feel restless. After an hour or so he
would switch the light back on and go online or try to
read a book. Sometimes he got up and went downstairs
for a glass of water, lingering in the kitchen or living
room while he drank it, always careful not to make any
noise that might wake up Sarah or the children, asleep in
their own rooms. When he did sleep, he dreamed vividly
and incoherently, though in the morning he could never
remember the details, just an echoing mood of anxiety
or elation.

All this was a consequence, it seemed clear, of his
listless and uneventful days, his unexercised mind and
body seeking an outlet or some kind of stimulation.
But the less he slept at night, the longer he napped
in the middle of the day – when sleep would overtake

him almost without warning – and the less he slept the following night, and so on.

One night, a Friday, when in fact he had fallen asleep easily, James woke up abruptly at around 1 a.m., his mind alert and with the strong sense that he would not be able to get back to sleep. He had been dreaming, and on this occasion he did remember the dream. He was at a residents' meeting in a house he didn't recognise, but instead of William, Vanessa, Kit and the other committee members sitting around the table there was Sarah, Greg and Connie Fuller, his manager Deborah, Rebecca Moffat, the runner who had tripped in front of him in the woods, dressed in his Lycra, his face still bleeding, and a bearded man dressed in brown robes whom he understood to be Matthews the Hairyman. James was no longer the chair but was being tried for some sort of act or crime, the details of which were not clear. Rebecca Moffat was smiling and saying the word 'chronic' over and over again. Just as the verdict was about to be delivered, Sidney the dog rushed in and dumped a lump of raw meat into James's lap. At that point he had woken up.

He lay in bed for a few minutes, turning the dream over in his mind, then got up and, without switching on the light, raised the blind. A car was parked opposite the house, just in front of the entrance to the woods. It was a Japanese make, James thought, black, or nearly black, customised so that it sat very low to the ground, with oversized wheels and spoilers on the front and back, presenting the appearance, at least, of speed and power. He did not recognise it, and although his neighbours sometimes had visitors, they did not usually drive cars like this. He had not noticed it there before he went to bed and he wondered if it was the sound of it pulling up that had woken him.

James stood at the window watching the car but the interior was dark and nothing happened. After a few minutes he pulled on his trousers and a T-shirt and went downstairs and out the front door. The night was warm and there was a slight breeze that rustled the leaves in the trees and carried the smell of the woods – mulchy, rotten, a little sweet. He approached the car slowly, picking his way carefully across the road in his bare feet. There was no moon and the nearest streetlight was twenty or thirty yards away, so he was very close to the car before his eyes adjusted to the dark and he was able to make anything out. When he did, it was more or less as he had expected.

They were in the backseat, the boy – it was hard to tell in the light, but James felt sure he was only a boy – facing forwards and the girl straddling him, her knees bent up on the seat. His trousers and pants were pulled down, exposing pale and hairless thighs and knotting his legs together around the knees. She was young too, anywhere between fifteen and eighteen, James thought, and wearing a dress that was now pushed up over her waist and down over her bra. Her thighs, wrapped around his, were pale too, and dimpled, the skin rougher and darker as it disappeared into her groin. The boy's face was buried in the crook of her right shoulder, concealed from James, but hers, facing forward, was caught in profile and strangely illuminated in the relative darkness, as if lit from some other source.

There was an urgency, even desperation, to their movements as they shifted their weight around to find a better position, a better fit. The boy's hands struggled to unfasten her bra. Several times he tried to raise her up, to move her forwards or back, but her head was trapped against the low roof of the car and his legs against the seat in front. Despite this, the girl's face, from this angle, was expressionless, somehow neutral or unmoved. Her long hair, white-blonde but with a thick blue streak down the middle, was swept over to the other side and James could see a faint down on her cheek and along the line of her jaw.

They began to move more easily now, to find a rhythm, and as James watched she gradually turned her head. Her eyes – made up in black liner that extended them out, cat-like, into points or wings on either side of her face – settled on James, standing no more than an arm's length away on the other side of the car door, peering in.

James stopped himself from crying out in surprise.

He was not mistaken. She was looking at him, without any apparent shock or alarm, as if she had entirely expected it. As James tried to take this in – that it was he and not she who had somehow been caught out – and even as the rest of her body moved and shook around her, her gaze did not shift nor her expression change except for the occasional slow blinking of her eyes. And as the seconds passed, something in its steadiness, its frank and unrelenting intensity, seemed to imply some kind of challenge. But what? To intervene and stop them? To look away? To carry on watching? Something else?

James could not say how long he had stood there, a few minutes he supposed. He felt the breeze on his neck, the warmth of the road under his feet. An owl hooted in the woods, then another seemed to answer it. He turned, walked across the road and let himself back into the house. A few minutes later, when he was still standing in the kitchen, he heard a car pull away.

6

IT WAS THE DAY OF THE NEW GLADES ESTATE summer party.

Soon after 7 a.m. the children began to run around downstairs. As James lay in bed exhausted, the morning sun glowing along the edges of the blind, the events of the night before had already acquired a peculiar quality. The whole thing seemed unlikely. Waking suddenly, going out without his shoes on, standing there in the dark, staring at the girl through the car window while she stared back at him. It was like something from a bad pornographic film. He thought again of his dream about the committee meeting. Had he simply woken from one dream into another? But if he closed his eyes, he could still see her vividly – her eyes, the mole, the pene-trating, hard-to-read expression. Regardless, he couldn't think about it any more now. He had a long, probably difficult day ahead of him, with no opportunity to catch up on lost sleep, and he resolved to put it out of his mind.

It was James's first party as chair of the residents' committee and he wanted it to be a success. At midday he went out of the back-garden gate to the shared land between the bottom terrace of the estate, where his own house was, and the one above, and started to set up. This was where they always held the party, an area known to the residents as The Field. The Field was the largest of the communal spaces on the estate, a kind of meadow rising up the incline of the hill, encircled on three sides by houses and on the fourth by the woods, entirely cut off from the road. The grass was allowed to grow a little longer here, and at this time of year drifts of buttercups, daisies and dandelions appeared almost overnight. Among the huge original old spruce were clusters of hornbeam and larch, knotty blackberry bushes and patches of nettles.

The Field was another perk of New Glades. The previous year, Laura had started to go out there on her own to be with her friends. She stayed out for hours, climbing in the trees, building dens, making up elaborate games. From inside the house, with the back door open, James could hear her shouts and calls and know she was never too far away from him and Sarah, or from the parents of the other children. It was, he had discovered, one of the great conundrums of parenthood, to give your children freedom without putting them at risk, to protect them without smothering them. At some point, not too long from now he supposed, Laura and her friends would be old enough to roam around the woods themselves, but until then The Field was a near-perfect solution. There was always a certain amount of anxiety when they were out of sight – that they would slip and hurt themselves, cut themselves on a branch or a bush, or even fall out of a tree – but overall, as Sarah had said to James with a wry smile, it seemed like 'just the right amount of freedom'.

On one of those first warm days of the year, just after the appearance of his palsy, James had been standing at an upstairs window when he saw Laura dart out of the back door, across the garden and up to the gate. He watched her as she opened it, looked quickly around and then broke into a run across the grass, her legs and arms swinging wildly, hardly coordinated, and he was overwhelmed by a kind of vicarious joy, even envy, for her, her thoughtless, surging vitality. Now that Sammy was walking, James took him out there too, and held his hand while he stumbled through the grass and picked clumsily at the daisies. In time Sammy would be out there with Laura, running alongside her or perhaps a little behind, trying to keep up, while James watched them both from the window.

William and Kit arrived in The Field soon after James and together they set up tables for the food and drink and pitched a gazebo for extra shade. After the abrupt ending of the previous committee meeting, James had made the arrangements over email. It was not complicated but did require everyone on the committee to do their bit and he had gone through everything meticulously during the week. The main concern was always the weather, but it had been fine for weeks and the forecast was for another hot day.

Greg had organised for a whole pig to be spit-roasted at the party. He had visited a farm, selected the animal himself, some kind of rare breed, and then helped slaughter it. He had sent James a detailed email about it earlier in the week, how, as he had prepared to fire the bolt gun between its eyes – the most humane method, apparently, which also preserved the best quality of the meat – the pig had looked up at him from under its long lashes. 'It was a profoundly intimate moment,' Greg had written, 'as intimate a moment as you can have with another living thing, I think. He knew exactly what was about to happen and I felt that he saw deep into me and me into him. We understood each other and I was very moved. And then I killed the bastard!' They had hung it by its back legs, drained the blood via the neck, skinned it and sawn off the head. James had found all this information too much and had not replied to the email, but when the man from the farm arrived and Greg helped him carry the pig down the hill and set it up over the spit, he had to admit that it would add something to the party.

Two more men arrived with a bouncy castle and, after conferring with James about where it should go, started to blow it up. Three residents who played together in a folk band set up their instruments and a PA system. It felt good to be active, discussing and giving instructions, even working up a sweat under the bright sun, and James forgot his tiredness. It was remarkable, he thought, how normal life could be. The parakeets had migrated from the cherry tree in front of the Orrs' house and settled in the tallest spruce, and they shrieked and twitched their scarlet beaks urgently, as if presiding over the preparations.

Around four o'clock the party began in earnest. The warm air had thickened with the smell of the roasting pig and Greg began to hack at it with a long knife he had bought specially for the occasion. Music was pumped through the PA system from someone's iPod. By five there was a good crowd, perhaps seventy or eighty people, the best they'd ever had, William said. This was down to the good weather, of course, but James felt his organisation could take some credit, too. The adults stood around in groups or sat on the grass and ate and drank and talked, while Kit ran games for the younger children. He had volunteered to do this – only someone without children would be naïve enough to offer, James had thought at the time – but he had organised them with a kind of military discipline and sharp blows of a whistle that the children seemed to respond well to. Around seven, the band began to play. James had never heard them before and, again, he was pleasantly surprised. A few people gathered at the front and danced, including Connie Fuller, wearing a long denim dress that flattered her figure and exposed her back and shoulders.

Finally, when he was satisfied that the party was running itself and there was nothing more for him to do, James went over to the spit-roast and asked Greg to fill a baguette for him.

'Is this what we can expect in France?' said James.

Greg looked at him.

'When we go away, I mean.'

'Oh right, absolutely.' Greg brandished his knife and grinned. 'Every night!'

James sat down under a tree to eat. He was now aware of a deep fatigue lurking just behind the adrenalin that had kept him going all day on little sleep and no nap. He looked around. He sensed a sort of settling and loosening in the mood, that small talk, awkwardness and neighbourly formality had given way to something more natural and uninhibited. No doubt many of them were a little drunk. James hadn't been drinking himself – it hadn't been agreeing with him since the beginning of the palsy – but he was happy to see everyone else having a good time, and to think that he had something to do with it.

The pork was extremely good, tender and crumbly, and James realised that it was the first thing he had eaten all day, that he had somehow neglected to have breakfast or lunch. He could hear Greg now, just above the music, telling Kit the same story about slaughtering the pig – 'And then I killed the bastard!' – and Kit's laughter. Throughout the afternoon James had noticed the familiarity between them. In the past, James and Greg had enjoyed disparaging Kit together – the ceaseless DIY, the lack of any obvious employment – and it was faintly disappointing now to see them apparently on such good terms. A few yards away, Sidney, the Fullers' dog, was wolfing down a plate of food that he had snatched from somewhere. This was a little annoying, too. Dogs were barred from the event, as the Fullers well knew, for exactly this sort of reason. There was a tennis ball lying at James's feet so he picked it up and threw it at Sidney, but it missed and bounced next to his head. The dog turned indifferently towards James for a moment and then went back to his food.

Sarah had walked over to James, holding Sammy's hand.

'Good party, Mr Chairman,' she said.

James nodded, his mouth full.

'Can you keep an eye while I go to the loo? See if he'll eat something.'

Sammy sat down on the grass and began to chew on a piece of the pork that James offered him. He had thick white-blond hair, as James had as a child, which fell in a natural bowl around his head. It had grown long through the spring and needed a cut, but Sarah said she could not bring herself to do it.

From day one Sammy had been a different personality to Laura. He was affectionate, sweet-natured and eager to please but terribly sensitive. If he felt that this affection was not being returned or that he was being told off, even if this was not the case, he became inconsolable. From time to time, and often on the thinnest pretext – a perceived slight from Laura, perhaps, whose manner could appear sharp or dismissive – he had screaming, red-faced tantrums which went on for minutes at a time and from which he could not be talked down. James wondered if this fragility was just a phase and would wear off over time, or whether it was something more essential to his nature and which he might carry with him through childhood and into adulthood. He hoped for Sammy's sake that it was the former. At the very least, he would learn to control or conceal these extremes. This, after all, was the whole meaning of growing up.

For these reasons, he supposed – though he felt guilty even admitting it to himself – he felt a tenderness towards his son, a kind of melancholy, sometimes quite painful, that he did not towards Laura, whose increasing self-sufficiency and apparent robustness put her slightly out of reach. Perhaps it was also to do with the simple fact of his being a boy, that he inescapably reminded James of himself. Sometimes, just to look at Sammy, as he did now, chewing tentatively on the piece of pork, his shining hair flopped over his eyes, caused a tightening in James's chest.

The band had finished. Kit blew the whistle he had been wearing around his neck all afternoon and announced that it was time for the football match.

The match was a tradition at the summer party, over-18s versus under-18s. It had become a sort of centrepiece to the day and, as James had discovered when he played the year before, it was surprisingly competitive. He had not planned to play this time around because of his organisational responsibilities and because of the palsy, but as it turned out, the over-18s, captained by Greg, were a man short. Without being asked, and rather to his own surprise, James put down his half-finished baguette, stood up and called out, 'I'm in.'

A member of the committee had been out the previous afternoon and mown a large rectangle in the longer grass, over towards the woods, to serve as a pitch. Someone else had provided plastic goals. There were eight of them in each team, ranging in age from Ben Fuller, Greg and Connie's eleven-year-old, through to William, somewhere in his sixties. The adults had changed their shoes and put on tracksuit bottoms or shorts. Several of the under-18s were in a complete team strip. Other residents had begun to gather along the edge of the pitch to watch. Kit stood in the centre, holding the ball.

'Twenty minutes each way, friends,' he said. 'Let's keep it clean.'

James was tired. He had eaten a total of half a baguette all day. He was wearing jeans and sandals and had a patch over one eye. He had, aside from his walks in the woods, been largely inactive for over a month. And yet, when Kit blew the whistle and Greg launched the ball towards where he was standing over on the right wing, James collected it neatly and began to run with it at his feet. Someone came sliding in towards him and he knocked the ball forward and skipped past the challenge. He weaved past another player and found himself suddenly – it was a small pitch – a few yards in front of the goal, with no one between him and the keeper, a lanky teenager he vaguely recognised from around the estate. Greg had run in on the other side and was shouting at James to cross the ball for a tap in, but, after only a moment's hesitation, James shifted his weight, dug his sandalled foot under the ball and chipped it over the goalkeeper's shoulder and into the net. Shouts went up from the spectators on the touchline.

It went on like this. James was everywhere on the pitch, sprinting the length and breadth of it to make a tackle, block a shot, receive a pass or jump for a header. He slotted the ball through other players' legs or slalomed past them with delicate touches. He called for the ball, shouted instructions to his teammates and exhorted them to work harder. As he ran, he felt the tiredness, not just of today, but of the enervated last few weeks, slough off him, like layers of packed earth. It was as if all the energy, all the vitality that had been drained from him over the past weeks had only been stored up somewhere else, and was now being released in a torrent. His body felt good, more than good: quick, agile, full of potential.

But it was not just energy. Even when he was younger and played regularly, he was of mediocre ability, and he had not so much as kicked a ball since the party the previous year. Now, though, everything went for him. He could pick the ball out of the air and bring it instantly under his control. He could play a long pass and deliver it exactly to a teammate's feet. When he dribbled it around the opposition the ball seemed magnetised to his feet. The other team were young, of course, but the sixteen- and seventeen-year-olds were big enough, and fast, too. Ben Fuller, the youngest on the field, with his name printed on the back of his replica shirt, could certainly play. The year before they had made James look flat-footed and old, and it was not unsatisfying to be showing them something different now.

His mind, it seemed, his one seeing eye and his body were unified, a single organism thrumming with alertness, and working at lightning speed, faster than anyone else on the pitch. The effect, from James's point of view, though, was to make his opponents, the whole game in fact, appear to move in a subtle slow motion, while he continued to act at normal speed, seeing the way the ball would run, the passes and tackles to be made, acting and reacting in a luxury of time. He had heard elite athletes describe something similar, this heightened state that could be achieved occasionally when they were at the very top of their game. He scored two more goals, one with his weaker left foot and one with his head. He thought of his family somewhere among the watching crowd, and was glad.

The problem was that James's teammates were not at the same level. The match had just a few minutes to play, it was three all, and despite his own efforts they were in danger of being overrun. The cumulative lack of fitness among the over-18s had begun to tell, as well as, James supposed, the alcohol that most of them had consumed. Greg was moving around the pitch at walking speed, the goalkeeper was sitting down between his posts and William had gone off altogether. In contrast, James felt he could go on forever, and, if anything, he had increased his intensity to compensate for the others. It was easier now to keep the ball himself rather than rely on the contribution of his teammates, and he continued to power his way up and down the field. Kit seemed to be blowing his whistle constantly, awarding fouls and free kicks, usually in the under-18s' favour, more for the sake of exercising his authority, James felt, than for any legitimate violations.

Then James made a mistake. It was overconfidence. He was at the halfway line, running with the ball, when he played it slightly too far ahead of himself. Ben Fuller was on it in an instant. He waited for a moment, and as James lunged to retrieve the ball, he knocked it around him, ducked around James the other way, picked up the ball and burst up the pitch towards the over-18s' goal. James turned and began to run after him. Ben was already several yards away and there were other teammates better placed to make an intervention, but it seemed clear to James that they no longer had the appetite for it.

James strained to make up the ground. Ben was not a big kid, perhaps a foot and a half shorter than James, but despite the difference in their stride, James wasn't catching him quickly enough. Ben was bearing down on goal – his bony, juvenile body, his oversized football boots, his shoulder blades jutting through his shirt either side of the large print of his name. The goalkeeper had staggered to his feet and was coming slowly, tentatively out towards him. A goal now, James saw, with barely any time to play, would be conclusive. It was too late to try and get around or ahead of him and so, with a final appeal to whatever resources he had in his system, James leant back, planted his feet an angle and slid in from behind.

The collision was awful, a tangling and crunching of limbs. Then, abruptly, James was lying on the ground, half on top of and half underneath Ben. The boy was crying forcefully and Greg was crouched over them both. A long, harsh note sounded very close to James's ears. He looked up and saw Kit above him. He had the whistle in his mouth and was staring down the barrel of it, holding his arm out straight and pointing James off the pitch.

The ball had rolled harmlessly away. He could see it over in the long grass. He had prevented the goal, but this, it was clear, was rather beside the point. He had hurt Ben, he did not know how badly. But as he got to his feet, the whistle still ringing in his ears, and looked over to the touchline for his family, James realised with a sickness that climbed immediately up into his throat that there was something even worse.

He had lost Sammy.

7

WHEN JAMES STOOD UP TO PLAY FOOTBALL HE
had simply – inexplicably – left Sammy sitting on the
ground. He had not given him to Sarah or asked anyone
else to watch him. He had not thought of him at all.

James could see immediately that Sammy was not
where he had left him, under the tree near where what
remained of the pig was still revolving slowly on its spit.
He could see Laura, distinctive in a yellow and orange
sundress, standing among a group of her friends, but
Sammy wasn't with her either.

He scanned the rest of The Field, looking for the
mop of hair, a small figure stumbling through the grass.
There were a few other children of a similar age but
none of them were Sammy.

'I've lost Sammy,' he shouted. 'Has anyone seen
my son?'

Somehow, throughout the game, he had imagined

that Sammy was there on the touchline with the others, with the rest of his family. Now it was clear that during all that time, more than half an hour, when James had been running around vainly, absurdly – this somehow made it all the more unforgivable – he was unaccounted for.

Anything could happen in half an hour. Up until a few weeks ago, they had only to worry about where Sammy might get to by shuffling awkwardly along on his bottom, and perhaps this went some way to explaining his complacency, James thought. But now that Sammy was up on his feet, his stumbling, rolling gait was surprisingly efficient. He, too, might not realise his new potential, how far and how fast his legs might take him. He might already have found his way past the houses and out onto the road. He might still be going, getting further away by the moment. Or, more likely, and knowing his son, Sammy would already feel lost and distressed.

James ran to the top of The Field to get a better view. The light had begun to fade during the game and the spruce trees were casting long shadows over the darkening grass. From here he could see that the party had thinned out a little, and the chatter seemed muted and desultory. The match had finished, or perhaps been abandoned. A cluster of people still stood around at one end of the pitch, the one where James had launched his tackle on Ben Fuller. The air was still and the smell of the spit-roast hung heavy and stale.

Although he had run only a short distance up the hill, fifty yards or so, from this perspective the scene below him, static and shrunken, had a shimmer of unreality about it. It was as if this were not New Glades itself but some intricate and fragile model of it and that all the things he saw – the trees and houses and people – were not these things, but representations of them. The model road wound smoothly through the terraces of miniature houses. There were model cars and intricately crafted gardens, model figures caught in some imitated pose or movement or gesture. Even the parakeets were there, high in the big tree, minutely small and obsessively detailed. The sun-streaked clouds had been painted artfully onto the background.

James himself had stepped out of the scene and he had the unnerving sense that if he could find a loose end and yank it sharply, it would shake free like a tablecloth, stretch taut and then concertina back together in a spasm, all its features, the trees and houses and cars and people, thrown into the air and then scattered carelessly across it. But of course all this was an illusion. The scene was real, emphatically and appallingly so, and somewhere in it – he did not know where – was his son.

'Sammy!' he called out. 'Sammy!'

James's eye swept over it again, left to right, and this time settled on the spit of trees and thick undergrowth that stuck out from the main body of the woods and formed a natural border to that side of The Field. For the most part, it was too dense to get into, but there was one overgrown path through it which, after fifty yards or so, opened into the larger part of the wood. He could see the entrance to the path now, a small, darker patch in the dark green of the trees, towards the bottom of the hill. What child, seeing that, James thought, would not walk towards it?

The torrential energy that had coursed through him on the football pitch now took hold of him in a different way, a second wind. James pushed and scrambled his way along the path, branches and leaves whipping at his face. He dropped to his knees to force his way under a fallen trunk. He thought of Sammy walking the same way, a few minutes earlier and in a different mood, his compact body easily negotiating the small gaps and constricted space, obstacles that might have been created precisely for his entertainment.

James emerged adjacent to the old train tunnel into the clearing where several of the larger tracks through the woods intersected. The canopy was high here but still thick, like the vaulted ceiling of a cathedral, and the light was dim. It was a place he knew well, but he had never been here at this time of day and, drained of colour and definition, it was unfamiliar and he found it hard to orientate himself. He paused for a moment, wondering which path to take, and felt the hush around him, as if the wood itself was waiting for him to act. He took the path straight in front.

Several times, as he ran, he tripped or stumbled over something on the ground, and only just managed not to fall. Gradually, as he got used to the surface and picked his legs up higher, he began to gather speed. He recognised individual things from his daytime walks – the outline of a particular thicket of trees, the dry bed of a stream, a rising bank, turns in the path – but he had little overall sense of where he was and no time, he felt, to stop and work it out. He thought of Sammy. Bare-armed, wearing his new shoes, a tiny anomaly among the massive trees, his hair glowing like a blond orb, walking into the darkness – afraid or oblivious to fear, and James did not know which of these was more terrible.

Soon, and without expecting it, he arrived back at the train tunnel. He had forgotten that the path looped around. Without stopping, he took the left path. The ground had been baked hard by weeks of sun and his knees ached. It was getting harder to pick his feet high up off the ground and it seemed only a matter of time before he went over. He heard the blood rushing in his ears and felt his heart in his chest, but he strained himself to keep going. It seemed to him that he was running to find Sammy, and to slow down or even stop would be to accept that the worst, the unthinkable, had already happened.

But then, just as he arrived back in the clearing in front of the train tunnel for a second time, his legs gave way completely and he fell to his knees. He vomited, bringing up the pitiful half-baguette he had eaten at the party. And as he did so, his hands planted in the earth in front of him, he knew, with the same conviction that moments before he had known Sammy was lost, that he had been safely at home with Sarah all along.

He retched several more times, painfully, but nothing else came up.

Part Three

I

JAMES KNELT ON THE GROUND FOR SOME TIME, immobilised. Eventually he stood up, and walked through the woods to the entrance opposite the front of his house. He loitered there in the shadow of the laurel hedge until he saw the lights in the children's bedrooms go out. Then he waited a little longer before crossing the road and climbing the steps to the house. Inside the porch he could hear the sound of the television from the living room and he closed the front door quietly and made his way straight upstairs. He pushed open Sammy's bedroom door and saw what he knew he would see, his son's small shape under the sheet in his cot, his head turned sideways under his hair, his arms thrown up above him. Then James went to the spare room.

The next morning he woke up in his clothes, physically wrecked. Every muscle in his body felt bruised, as if he had been beaten up. He had scratches on his face and hands and dirt and grit under his fingernails. There was a tear in his T-shirt and the taste of sick was still in his mouth. He stayed in bed until lunchtime, then had a shower and went apprehensively downstairs. Sarah was sitting at the kitchen table, with the laptop open.

'You had a late one,' she said, looking up. 'I didn't hear you come in. Probably just what you need.'

'What do you mean?' James said, anxiously.

'To have a few drinks. Talk to some people.'

James nodded. He had anticipated a row.

'I'm sorry I didn't stay out,' she said.

After using the toilet, Sarah explained, she had come out and found Sammy sitting on the steps in the back garden, chattering to himself. His nappy needed changing and it was already past his bedtime so she had taken him in, read him a story and put him to bed. After that, she had stayed in herself. Laura had come in sometime later. Sarah had not seen the football match that had culminated in James's crunching tackle on Ben Fuller or witnessed the hysteria that had sent him running into the woods in pursuit of Sammy. She did not even admonish him for leaving Sammy wandering alone in The Field. The completeness of James's neglect had apparently not even occurred to her.

'Oh shit,' Sarah said abruptly, and looked at her watch. 'We're supposed to be somewhere. Kids!' she shouted.

Five minutes later the door slammed and they had gone. James went back upstairs to the spare room and lay on the bed.

In many ways, the conversation with Sarah was a relief. He had acted bizarrely at the party, no doubt, but perhaps the damage was not as great as he had feared and anyway, when he replayed the day in his mind, there were mitigating circumstances. He had felt a lot of pressure for the party to go well. He had only had a couple of hours' sleep the night before, missed entirely the daytime nap he had become accustomed to, barely eaten, and it had been hot – not to mention the accumulated stress of the past months.

It was a disturbing lapse, of course, the way he had forgotten Sammy so completely before the football, but as Sarah's reaction suggested, by itself it was not the dreadful misdemeanour he had initially taken it to be. When he realised he had forgotten him, instead of taking the rational course of action and locating Sarah, he had compounded the mistake by panicking and running maniacally into the woods. In the end, nothing bad – nothing irrevocable – had happened. It was all just a case of over-reacting.

But still, something in what Sarah had said rankled with him. 'Probably just what you need,' she had said, 'to have a few drinks,' 'talk to some people'. Here it was again – like the suggestion that he take up a hobby – the implication that his current difficulties, the palsy and all that went with it, might simply be alleviated by getting out more or changing his habits, that it was all just something he could get over if he tried hard enough. It sometimes felt as if, from day one, she had not taken it – or him – entirely seriously. And yet, at the same time, she had indulged him. She had not pushed him to go back to work or queried why he was not helping out more at home. She had accepted his incapacity all too readily, worked around it without complaint. Previously, he had just thought that this was her way of coping – there was a good deal to cope with, after all – but she did not give the impression of someone who was only coping. If anything, she seemed to be thriving.

After an hour James got up and went round to the Fullers'.

For a long time after he knocked no one came to the door. He was just about to turn away, disappointed, when Connie opened it.

'James,' she said.

'Hi,' said James.

She hadn't opened the door very far. She was leaning on it with one shoulder and her other arm was raised in a right angle, her hand resting high up on the frame.

'I wanted to apologise for last night,' James said.

'Okay.'

'I was… I got carried away. Can I speak to Ben?'

Connie looked at him but said nothing. She was still wearing the denim dress from the night before. Her hair was a mess and she seemed drowsy, a little out of it, her green eyes a little unfocused behind her glasses. Perhaps she was hungover from the party or perhaps she had been asleep. James could see Sidney skulking in the porch behind her.

'He's out,' she said eventually. 'Everyone's out.'

'Right. Is he okay?'

Connie carried on looking at him, her head at a slight angle, as if it were she who had just asked a question and was waiting for his reply. He touched his face self-consciously.

'I got carried away,' he said again.

There was a long pause and then Connie said, 'I know you have been having a difficult time, James—'

'I have!' James said eagerly.

He was surprised by this, but pleasantly so. It was good of her to acknowledge it, and he felt a tremendous surge of gratitude. He smiled. He was standing very close to her, almost in the doorway himself. He followed the line of her angled arm, from her hand on the door frame, along the taut curve of her bicep, onto her bare freckled shoulder and then opening into the fine, clear structure of her collarbones and throat.

She had told him everyone was out. It was as if this act, his violent collision with Ben on the football pitch, had caused another kind of rupture, a brutal but necessary reordering of possibilities, the stripping away of previously maintained levels of inhibition and restraint. A whole new vista of understanding had opened up between them – and, with it, the chance of some even greater form of forgiveness or relief.

'I know you have been having a difficult time, James,' Connie said, and James was not sure if she had repeated this, or if it was simply the echo of her words in his head. She released her hand from the door frame and for a moment it seemed as though she were going to reach out and touch his face, the palsied side, to lay her hand on it – but she did not. She placed it in the middle of his chest and pushed him sharply, so that he tripped and stumbled backwards, only just staying on his feet.

'But this is not okay,' she said and closed the door.

2

ON THURSDAY NIGHT, THERE WAS A MEETING OF
the residents' committee. This was standard procedure,
an opportunity to debrief and tie up any loose ends from
the party, but James, who had not left the house all week
except for the brief, unsatisfactory visit to the Fullers on
Sunday afternoon, had not been looking forward to it.
In the event, it did not go well.

James had prepared some opening remarks for the
meeting, to the effect that the party had been a great
success and everyone on the committee could be proud
of their own contribution. He hoped to get through the
evening quickly and without any disasters like the spon-
taneous welling up of his eye that had sabotaged the last
one, but he had only just begun to speak when William
interrupted him.

'I think it would be better to get this out of the way
straight off the bat, as it were.' He paused, took the lid

off the pen he was holding, then put it back on. 'James, you are to be relieved of the chair's role, I'm afraid, effective immediately.'

'Excuse me?' said James.

'You aren't the chair any more, James,' said Vanessa, not kindly.

They were meeting at Vanessa's house. It was the first time James had been there and there was an unmistakably psychedelic feel to the décor. A vast sunburst tie-dye hung from one wall, and on the others were images of elephants, Buddhas and Indian gods with many arms. They were all sitting, rather uncomfortably as far as James was concerned, on beanbags and cushions around a low table in the centre of the room.

'Well, I'm not sure what you mean,' said James. 'Apart from anything else, the constitution of the committee does not permit…'

'On the contrary,' William continued, sliding one of the pairs of glasses hanging around his neck onto his nose and looking down at the notes in front of him, 'it states explicitly that if a majority of the committee believe that the chair can no longer be deemed fit to hold the position then a vote of no confidence automatically removes him – or her – from office. You wrote these regulations yourself.' He held up a piece of paper and flapped it in the air. 'That vote took place before you arrived this evening.'

It was a bureaucratic coup, a stitch-up. James looked around the room at the rest of the committee. Only Vanessa met his eye, unrepentantly. Was this to do with his behaviour at the party? Another thought went through his mind, that somehow they knew about the couple in the car and how James had stood and watched them and then failed to mention it to anyone. He had the sudden image of someone – who? – standing at a window or on a porch in the darkness, watching him watching them.

'No longer deemed fit?' James said. 'May I ask on what basis?'

'We have received a complaint. In fact, a number of complaints.'

'From who?'

'I am not at liberty to share that information, I'm afraid.' William paused and then went on: 'In retrospect it would perhaps have been better for you not to have taken the role in the first place, without proper consultation. But you were very insistent. A lesson for all of us about the importance of process, I think.'

'But I didn't—'

'Have some dignity, James,' said Vanessa.

She was right. What was the point of protesting further? It was over, a fait accompli. James looked around at the committee and for a prolonged moment he felt the same dislocation he had experienced when he stood at the top of The Field and surveyed the estate below as he looked for his lost son. This time it was the image of his neighbours, the committee, squatting awkwardly around the too-low table that struck him as just some brittle veneer on reality, one that might fracture or shatter entirely at any time. There was a sudden loud laugh, almost a shriek, but it was not clear who it had come from, and then the room was silent again.

'James,' William went on, 'let me take this opportunity to note our thanks to you for all your work on behalf of the committee and the association. We would welcome your continuing participation as an ordinary member of the committee and the experience that you bring, but of course understand completely if, under the circumstances, you would prefer not to attend in future.'

James was barely listening now. Everything had an air of inevitability, as if he were watching a film he had seen many times before.

'Kit has kindly agreed to take on the chair's responsibilities temporarily, as of this evening, until we can organise an election and make a more permanent appointment. I know he has some exciting ideas.'

William looked up and nodded at Kit. James looked over at him too. He was sitting in his beanbag with his hands clasped together and resting on the table in front of him. His expression was impassive but he nodded faintly when William mentioned his name, as if the acceptance of this responsibility was an extremely sober matter. He had not spoken throughout the meeting, but of course he didn't need to.

The meeting moved on to other matters. James listened vaguely to the discussion – about the CCTV cameras, the gardening and maintenance contract, plans for a bonfire night party in the autumn – things that no longer seemed to have much to do with him. Then, after a few minutes, and with some difficulty, he pushed himself up from the beanbag, packed his papers in his bag and, for the second time in as many meetings, left early.

3

JAMES WAS STILL NOT SLEEPING WELL. HE EXPECT-
ed to get little more than two or three hours a night
now, and usually not until towards dawn. Nevertheless,
he carried on going to bed at his usual time, in the hope
that that particular night might be different. When, after
an hour or so, it was not, he would get up, pull up the
blind and stand looking out of the window at the estate
and the woods beyond. He looked along the laurel
hedge that bordered the woods, the pools of sodium
light around the streetlamps, the procession of neat
front gardens that led away to the bend in the road. He
was half-looking, he supposed, for unfamiliar cars pulled
up silently in the shadows, though what he would do if
he saw one, he did not know.

He brooded. The residents' meeting was a humilia-
tion, undeniably, but really, what did it matter? Despite
what William had said – and this idea that James had

been 'very insistent' about chairing the committee was absurd – he had never wanted the job anyway. It would be a weight off him not to have to deal with the tedious administration and petty politics that went with it. No, it was not this that he brooded on now but Sarah, or, more precisely, his and Sarah's relationship – the separate beds, the silly things he had not told her about, the distance between them, his passivity in allowing all this to occur. And the more he thought about it, night after night, the clearer it became that over the last weeks and months he had been preoccupied with precisely the wrong things. He had inflated the trivial and diminished the important. He had got everything terribly wrong.

On one of these nights, a few days after the residents' committee meeting – a few days when he had seen Sarah and the children barely at all – when he had already lain awake for several hours and then stood for some time at the window, he went to the bathroom to use the toilet before trying again to get to sleep. He stood to wash his hands and looked up at the mirror above the sink. He thought of the first morning of the palsy (how long ago was that now? Three months? He had lost track) when he had stood in the same place, with Sarah next to him, and contemplated his transformed face.

There was the beard now, bushy, fully gingery, in need of a trim. His hair was nearly down to his shoulders, longer than he had ever had it. As it grew, the curl had come through, but now the weight of it was pulling it flat and straight against his head. Perhaps he should think about tying it back. And there was the patch, too, which he rarely took off.

James tried to smile. The right side of his mouth pulled back over his teeth and he grimaced in the mirror. He pulled the left side up to match the right, then dropped it back down. He watched as he ran his finger slowly down the left side of his face and still he felt nothing. He pushed back the patch. His eye, red and inflamed, stared back at him and he had an urgent sense of what he should do.

James pushed open the bedroom door with his finger-tips. It was dark, just a little moonlight coming through a gap in the blind, but he could make out the rough shape of Sarah's body, the rise of her hips and then her shoulders, under the sheet. She was towards the left side of the bed, where she had always slept when James was in there with her. She was lying on her right-hand side, the sheet pulled up to her chin, her hair spread on the pillow. Her hands were flat against each other and wedged under her cheek, in a way that seemed almost posed. Her jaw had dropped a little, opening her mouth, and she was snoring gently. It had been weeks, months now, since

James had seen her like this, he realised, and the thought of this – that the sight of his sleeping wife had become so unfamiliar – overwhelmed him for a moment.

He walked round to the other side of the bed, his side. There was a little table there, pushed against the wall, which had some of his things on it, his watch, a book he had been reading but forgotten about. He slipped off his pants and T-shirt, took hold of the corner of the sheet and pulled it back enough for him to slide in. Immediately, and without touching her, he could feel the heat coming off Sarah's body.

She stirred a little, and the snoring stopped. James lay still.

Now that he was here, he felt even more confident that this was the right thing to do. He had allowed himself to think that it was the palsy that had curtailed their sex life, accepted it as an inevitability, when in fact this lack long preceded his illness. After all, they had made love that first weekend and it had been fierce and satisfying. Thinking of that now, it was hard to see why they had not carried on from there. She had instigated it then and he had failed to instigate it since – and, thought of like this, her recent coolness towards him was actually a kind of provocation.

Sarah's snoring had resumed. James turned on his side, edged his way across the bed, and then lay, not touching her, but echoing her shape – back curved, bottom pushed out, legs bent ninety degrees at the knee. Her body seemed to sense this and shifted a little and then resettled, like a subtle, instinctual acknowledgment of his presence.

James breathed in, flexed his groin forward, and steered his erection between her buttocks. At the same time he reached his arm across her body, and cupped her left breast with his hand.

Sarah's body went rigid, and then, a moment later, she cried out and jerked away from him. James was alert and grabbed her wrists, forced them down on to the mattress, and straddled her with his legs.

'It's me,' he said, but the noise that came out of his mouth was mangled, incomprehensible even to himself. 'It's me, James,' he said again, clearer this time.

'James!' she said. 'What are you doing? Are you insane?'

'Midnight Rapist!' he said.

Even in the weak light he could see her expression – uncomprehending, aghast.

'Get off me, James! Get off!'

He held on to her wrists and didn't move.

'I said get off!'

She bucked her hips in the air violently and James was surprised at her strength – or his own lack of it. He held on but he had lost his balance and when she bucked again he was thrown off the bed sideways and onto the floor. Sarah reached out and switched on the lamp by the bed.

'Mummy?' said a voice behind James. He twisted his head round from where he lay, collapsed on the floor. Laura was silhouetted in the doorway.

'It's okay, darling, go back to bed,' Sarah said, her voice a little breathless but composed, 'it's just your father.'

4

JAMES DIDN'T GET BACK TO SLEEP. IN THE MORN-
ing he heard the rest of the family get up and begin to
move around the house. Around forty-five minutes later
he heard the front door as they went out. He stayed in
bed for another hour or so and then got up and went
downstairs. On an impulse he called his office, his own
extension. He let it ring twice, then had a different idea
and hung up.

It was strange to be on the train again. It was well past
rush hour, there had been no one else on the platform
and now he was alone in the carriage, too. He listened
to the familiar litany of station names announced over
the PA and leaned forward in his seat so as to better see
out of the window. James had always enjoyed this view
of the city, its face turned away from you, the backs of
houses, industrial units, lorry and train depots, recycling

plants. There were blocks of flats with tiny balconies crammed with bikes and barbecues and washing hung out to dry. Among these, one large block was missing an entire exterior wall, exposing perhaps ten floors of identically sized rectangular rooms, like a doll's house with the front opened up. Apart from the missing wall, these flats looked barely abandoned, each one brightly painted, forming an oddly beautiful patchwork. Most of them still contained furniture, shelves, beds and cupboards. It was not hard to imagine people moving around inside them.

At the third stop, a group of schoolchildren got into James's carriage. There might have been thirty of them, a little older than Laura he thought but not much, and they swarmed into the seats around him. The noise was startling, a squall of shouting, laughing and arguing, so self-consumed and oblivious to James that it was somehow surprising that they did not sit directly on top of him. They were all dressed for the weather, bare legs and arms, sandals, some with hats. James was in the heavy boots and mud-flecked jeans he wore to walk in the woods. On the way out of the house he had also grabbed an old black duffle coat with a hood that could be pulled across his face to better conceal the palsy. It had not seemed a problem as he marched purposefully through the shade and relative cool of the woods to the station, but now, in the hot, airless carriage, he was beginning to sweat.

There were two children squashed into the single seat next to him and every few seconds one of them elbowed him sharply in the ribs. Underneath the table the feet of the children opposite him kicked constantly against his ankles and shins. James tried to follow their conversations but they were so rapid and excitable that he found he could only pick out the odd word or phrase, like listening to one of the languages he had learned in school but mostly forgotten. Then, abruptly, the train pulled into the next station, the doors opened, and the children moved off with an odd bustling efficiency, like an insect colony sharing a single, collective intelligence. James listened to the hum of their voices retreating along the platform, the train doors closed, and he was alone again in the carriage.

The next station was the end of the line and James got off. Instead of heading into the Underground he decided to walk the rest of the way. It was not so far. He used to do it all the time – to cross the river and see the city stretching away grandly along the banks in either direction, to feel the air and collect his thoughts before arriving at work. But as he stepped outside the air-conditioned station concourse, the heat hit him like a wall. It was said that cities were hotter than other places, sometimes by several degrees – the density of people and buildings and traffic – and so it made sense that the nearer you got to the centre, the hotter it was. Around him now the sheer walls of shining steel and glass and white stone seemed to reflect and magnify the sun, concentrating its force, and he felt that if you touched any of these surfaces you might burn yourself. He looked at the people in shorts and sunglasses, sandals and trainers, open-neck shirts and T-shirts, and felt again the inappropriateness of what he was wearing.

Up on the bridge it was only a little better. The river was low, unusually so, grey-brown and barely flowing, and on either side of it were great banks of mud littered with the hulls of derelict barges. There was a faint breeze but it smelt bad, of stagnant water and drains. He looked upriver and down, but beyond a certain distance, not much further than the next bridge in either direction, everything was lost in a haze.

On the other side, James became disorientated. He had arrived at a junction different from the one he had expected, as if he had crossed the wrong bridge altogether. Here the roads forked, taking you left or right, when he had planned to walk straight on. In front of him, blocking the way, was a large asymmetrical building that jutted up and out at various sharp angles. The façade was of some odd textured or pummelled metal that appeared to wobble or vibrate very rapidly in the heat. James had no memory of seeing the building before, or even of a construction site in this spot, but this was not entirely surprising. For as long as he had been coming to this part of the city it had been in the grip of a remorseless redevelopment, cranes and temporary boardings and scaffoldings and planned diversions. A testament to its vitality, James had always thought, although now it did not feel so benign.

Unwilling to stop or go back, James pressed on left, the way that felt the least wrong, but now none of it seemed familiar. It was broadly the same place that he knew so well, the same essential variety of architectural styles and periods, the same chains of shops and cafés and restaurants, the same grammar of signs and traffic lights and roads and people, but none of it fitted together in the right way, like an incorrectly assembled jigsaw. He walked on like this for some time, never slowing down, refusing to stop and ask for directions or to try and properly orientate himself. At some point, he felt, he must see something that made sense, an arrangement of buildings or roads, an unmistakable sign that he knew where he was. The heat was horrendous. He could feel sweat pooling under his clothes. He could take off the duffle coat but he did not want to stop, and anyway he would only have to carry it under his arm and this did not seem much better. He was tremendously thirsty but he had not thought to bring a bottle of water with him and, he realised, had no money to buy one.

And then he did see something, a tiny medieval building crammed between two much larger modern office blocks. He had never been in it – some kind of church or chapel – but it was unmistakable, a part of the everyday scenery of his days at work. With renewed confidence he crossed the road and entered the building next to it.

Inside, it was more or less as he remembered. The high, bright atrium, the polished wooden floor, the collection of leather sofas and chairs for visitors to wait in, the glass curve of the reception desk and the bank of lifts to one side and the stairs to the other. James turned and began to walk towards the lifts but somebody stepped in his way.

'Sir?'

James had made a habit, when he was working, of getting to know all the security guards' names and exchanging a nod or a word with them when he came and went from the building. It was basic politeness. This one, however, he did not know, although given the time he had been away, this, again, was not particularly surprising.

'Can I see your ID, sir?'

James patted the pockets of his duffle coat, and then held up his hands.

'I haven't got it with me, I'm afraid.'

'May I ask who you are here to see, sir?'

'I work here. Or at least, I do usually – I haven't been…'

'Sir, if I can ask you to step over here with me.'

The guard – John, his name badge said – took James by the arm.

'That won't be necessary,' James said, and planted his feet further apart to better balance himself. He gave the guard the name of his firm but this produced no reaction. It occurred to him that it was the sound of his voice that was the problem. He had got used to it himself, the slight mangling and slur of what he was trying to say, but he had forgotten how hard it was for other people to understand him. He pulled back his hood.

'I apologise. I am not making myself clear. I have a small issue with my mouth.'

He repeated the name of his firm, more slowly this time, enunciating the sounds carefully, and then gave Deborah's name as well, but still this did not seem to register. Was it possible that the firm had changed its name? This had happened once before when they merged with another company. Could it have moved offices? These things were possible, but they did not happen overnight, and surely he would have been informed? What about Deborah, his manager and mentor? Could she have left the company? This seemed more plausible – she was ambitious, after all – and perhaps he just hadn't caught up with the news.

'Would it help if I wrote it down?'

Another security guard had arrived – Robert, this one was called – and he felt the first one's grip tighten at his elbow. He thought of his colleagues up on the top floor, ten short steps and a lift ride away from where he was now, sitting at their desks, standing talking in the kitchen or perhaps all together in the meeting room, his own empty desk by the window.

James felt a familiar dampness on his left cheek and he reached up to touch it with his fingers.

'Excuse me,' he said and pushed the patch up on to his forehead. The tears that had gathered under it rolled down his face. 'It's not what you are thinking. I am not crying. If you look, the tears are only coming out of one eye. They are tears but I am not crying. It's only one eye!'

At that moment James saw, crossing the atrium towards the lifts, a familiar figure – a familiar walk, a familiar haircut and carrying a handbag he recognised too. She had not left the company after all, and the company had not moved. He tried to move forward but his arms were locked tight against the security guards.

'Deborah!' he shouted. 'Deborah!'

'Time to go, sir,' said one of the guards, and James felt himself lifted ever so slightly off the ground between them and then turned around. They started to walk him back towards the entrance, his feet gliding weightlessly over the polished floor. He twisted his neck around to look back over his shoulder.

'Deborah!' he shouted one more time. 'It's me, James Orr!' Finally the woman had turned around and was looking at him curiously across the atrium.

It was not Deborah. Of course it was not.

5

LATER, AT HOME, JAMES TRIED TO NAP. HE HAD been awake since dawn the previous day. The trip into town had been traumatic and exhausting. He remembered being escorted from the building by the security guards, but after that everything was a blur. Somehow, apparently, he had found his way home and now the most important thing seemed to be to get some sleep. Normally, he did not find this difficult in the daytime, but Kit was cutting lengths of wood on a workbench set up on the pavement outside his house and every time James felt he was about to drift off, the rasp of the saw – so loud that it seemed to be there in the room, next to his head – jolted him awake. He tried in the spare room, then on the sofa downstairs, but wherever he was the sound seemed to follow him and eventually he gave up.

Outside, James went quickly down the steps and

across the road to avoid being seen, but as soon as he was through the gate in the laurel hedge and into the woods he dropped his pace. He had walked through there earlier in the day, to and from the station, but on the way he had been thinking only of getting to work and he remembered almost nothing about the journey back. Before that it was nearly two weeks since he had been in the woods, the night he had run around in a panic looking for Sammy, and straightaway he saw – and felt – that everything had changed. It was as if, in his short absence, and even though it was still early summer, the year had peaked and spent itself. It had been hot and dry for so long that the leaves had already begun to wilt and lose their colour. The grasses were trodden down and the paths were hard and dusty. The birdsong was muffled and listless. The flowers were all gone but for an unfamiliar violet-coloured weed that had sprung up wherever he looked. The air was thick and soupy and the light seemed to blur the edges of everything.

This did not dismay James, it was just part of the natural cycle after all. After the growth and vigour of the first part of the year, other forces had set in, of decline and decay. And as he walked – up and past the old foundations, down along the dried-up stream bed, alongside the bleached fairways of the golf course, the echoless crack of balls being struck in the dead air – he felt his exhausted and inflamed senses attune themselves power-fully to the momentum of this great and subtle process. He stopped and peeled a strip of desiccated bark as long as his arm from the trunk of a birch tree. He watched a leaf drop from a hawthorn bush and he caught it in his hand. In every direction the unfamiliar weed was spreading out ahead of him.

He did not know how long or how far he had walked in this exalted state when he turned onto a path and saw, fifteen yards or so ahead of him, a large animal blocking the way. It was Sidney, the Fullers' dog. Strictly speaking the trust's rules did not allow dogs off the lead in the woods – there were signs at every entrance – let alone unaccompanied, as Sidney appeared to be now. Still, it was not so surprising to see him there. No doubt he had bolted out of the Fullers' front door or jumped the back-garden fence, as he had many times before.

Sidney himself gave no sign of being anywhere he shouldn't be. He was rooting around in the bushes at the edge of the path, following a scent or perhaps, James thought, deciding on somewhere to do one of his enor-mous shits. He hadn't noticed James. Even at a distance, James was struck, as he always was, by just how big this animal was. He was a good four foot high, perhaps six when he was up on his back legs, his paws were barely smaller than James's own hands and he might easily weigh ten stone. James knew that he cost the Fullers a fortune in food. From somewhere the sun was penetrating the woods and catching in his wiry grey coat and he stood ahead of James in the middle of the path in massive, glowing outline.

James had stopped to observe Sidney but now he stepped forward. The dog sensed him – saw or smelt or heard him – and immediately, but unhurriedly, turned and lifted his head, his huge grey eyes, to look at James. It was a look of utter indifference. He registered no surprise or alarm at seeing James there on the path but nevertheless held his gaze, blinking slowly, blandly, as James continued to approach. Then, when James was around six feet away, Sidney turned his head away and, without shifting the position of the rest of his body on the path, began once again to forage in the bushes.

A small log, around two feet long and as thick as James's leg, lay to one side of the path. He picked it up with both hands, raised it in the air, and took two more steps forward. At the last moment, the dog withdrew his head from the bushes and turned again to look at James. Again, their eyes met and James recognised the feeling Greg had described in the slaughterhouse when he prepared to fire the bolt gun, a profound intimacy, a communion of souls. *And then I killed the bastard*, he thought.

It was easier than he might have expected. James caught him well the first time, precisely between the eyes, and felt something give, the skull he supposed. Sidney's eyes widened a little, his nostrils flared and his ears seemed to prick up, as if in some final rush of sensory awareness. Then his legs gave way, feebly, not so much from the force of the blow but as if from some command – or failure of command – from the animal's brain and he toppled, massively, into the bushes, dragging branches down with him, the flattened undergrowth cushioning the sound. James stood over the body and brought the log down three more times on the dog's head. It hardly seemed necessary. Underneath him, he felt Sidney draw in a sharp breath, like a gasp, release it slowly – and then nothing.

6

IT HAD RAINED OVERNIGHT AND EVERYTHING
felt rinsed clean and fresh. Kit was outside his house.
After weeks of sawing and sanding, he had begun to glue
and nail the wood together to make the new window
frames. Two days ago the glass had been delivered in a
van and the driver had helped Kit secure it in the frames
and then lift them into place on the house. Now Kit was
balanced halfway up a ladder, wearing only shorts and
workmen's boots, applying a layer of white paint.

After a while, Greg came out of the Fullers' house
next door, also in shorts and wearing a straw hat and
sunglasses, and carrying a suitcase in each hand. He
called out to Kit, Kit shouted something back, and they
both laughed. Greg unlocked the car, put the cases in
the boot and went back inside. For the next half hour
he came and went, carrying more suitcases, bags, a cooler
box, boxes of food, a football, tennis rackets. When the

boot was full he opened the box on top of the car and filled that, too. Then he fixed the children's bikes to a rack on the back. Eventually the children came out, the older two in front, the little one trailing behind, and got into the car. Last came Connie, also in sunglasses. She pulled the door shut and then locked it. Kit had come down the ladder and he rubbed his hands on his shorts and shook hands with Greg and kissed Connie on both cheeks. Greg and Connie got into the car, Kit banged his fist twice on the roof and they drove off, slowly at first, and then faster.

At the top of the hill, where the estate road met the main road, a van was parked. Large letters on the side of the van read 'Expert Security Solutions' and gave a website address and phone number. Two men in hard hats and high-visibility orange vests had assembled a scaffolding platform adjacent to the first house on the estate road and were standing on top of it to secure a pair of cameras to the wall, one pointing in each direction. After a while William came out of his house opposite with two cups of tea and a packet of biscuits on a tray. The men took off their hats, took the tea and sat in the open back of the van to drink it. William stayed talking to them until they were finished and then carried the tray back inside.

Later on, when the light had turned dusky, James stood outside the front window of his own house, looking in through a gap in the blinds. The lights were on inside and the three of them, Sarah, Laura and Sammy, were sitting on the sofa. The children were in their pyjamas. They had both had their hair cut. Laura was wearing the headdress she had made from parakeet feathers and reading a book. Sammy was sitting on Sarah's lap, eating something out of a bowl and watching TV. It was as if James himself had just left the room for a moment, to get something from the kitchen perhaps or to go the toilet, and at any second he would reappear and sit down with the rest of his family.

Something caught Laura's eye and she glanced up from her book towards the window, but James ducked out of sight and went quickly down the steps.

In the folly, he had rearranged things a little. He had cleared the old ashes from the fire and there was a pile of fresh logs in the corner. He had removed several loose bricks from the wall to make a shelf, where he kept a pan and a mug. Now he swept the floor. He felt that it might rain again overnight and so he climbed the side of one of the walls and retied the tarpaulin at a better angle. There was a small tear in it and at some point, he thought, it would need patching. When he got down he took off his boots and put them in the corner next to the stove. He took off his shirt and trousers, put them on hangers and hung them from a branch. He passed his hand absently over the left-hand side of his face, then took out the sleeping bag, unrolled it and got in.

The air was cooler now but when he laid his head down he could smell the warm, swept earth. He looked up. Everywhere in the branches above were the vivid greens and yellows of the parakeets, their scarlet beaks, as if some florid blight had spread through the tree. The flock had grown since the beginning of spring, the birds had reproduced themselves or merged with another group, and there were more than he could count. The screeching had almost subsided now they were settled in to roost. James was tired, too. He closed his one good eye. He could hear faintly, very faintly, the hum of traffic on the main road and knew that before long he would be asleep.

Acknowledgements

GRATITUDE AND THANKS ARE DUE TO ALISTAIR Daniel, Maura Dooley, Ben Felsenburg, Cathryn Summerhayes, Laura Barber and everyone at Granta. Thanks and apologies to Jamie Johnson. Love and thanks to all the Lees, all the de Zoysas, and of course, and especially, the Lee de Zoysas.

I would also like to acknowledge the generous assistance of Arts Council England and the Royal Society of Literature's Brookleaze Grant, which enabled the writing of this book.